W9-AQO-023

Homeroom Exercise

Homeroom Exercise

JANA
STRIEGEL

Holiday House / New York

Library of Congress Cataloging-in-Publication Data
Striegel, Jana.
Homeroom exercise / by Jana Striegel.—1st ed.
p.   cm.
Summary: When twelve-year-old Regan begins to suffer from juvenile rheumatoid
arthritis, she must face the possibility that her dream of being a professional dancer may
never come true.
ISBN 0-8234-1579-1 (hardcover)
[1. Rheumatoid arthritis—Fiction. 2. Physically handicapped—Fiction.
3. Dance—Fiction.] I. Title: Homeroom exercise. II. Title.

PZ7.S91685 Ho 2002
[Fic]—dc21   00-033533

*For
my son, Tanner,
my sweet love and miracle child
and
my husband, Mark,
for believing—
in more ways than one*

Acknowledgments

I am grateful to Shelley Brobst and her mother, Ann Roux, whose candor and emotions pointed me in the right direction to tell this story. I extend my appreciation to Dr. William Benge, Dr. Eric A. Peters, and the Arthritis Foundation for their technical guidance about juvenile rheumatoid arthritis.

Thanks go to Denise Woody and her fifth-grade classes, middle school teacher Lorraine Andrews and assistant principal Debra Hamilton, to the organization SouthWest Writers, and to authors Janet Long Ford, Gayle Gardner, Elaine Greenspan, Madge Harrah, and Paula Paul for their wisdom and generous encouragement.

My talented editor, Regina Griffin, Holiday House, and my agent, George Nicholson, are on my angel list. Thank you.

And thank you to a group of people who sparkle in my life and provide unending support: Cheryl, Janie, Lois, Lyn, Paula, Shelly, David, Adrian, Renee, Lana, Lezlie, Amy, Kate, Katie, Betsi, Monica, Stefanie, Lara, Krista, Rich, Geoffrey, Roy, Jan, Rick, Ron, Caprice, and anyone else who never gives up.

Finally, *merci beaucoup* to all the dancers I have had the privilege to dance with and teach. Listen closely, and you will hear my own ballet fairies whispering within these pages.

Jana Striegel

Chapter One

Regan marked the ballet combination with her hands, using her fingertips for toes and her wrists for ankles. Sauté, tombé, pas de bourrée, double pirouette, land. Assemblé, entrechat trois, prepare fourth, spin spin, land. Then she danced it full out, spinning like a globe. She stuck the landing—yes! That one worked.

Regan moved her head to the music pumping from a boom box at the opposite side of the dance studio. Four girls surrounded the CD player as if it were a ceremonial fire. They swerved their hips through figure eights and chanted, "Oowa, oowa, oo-oo-oo, oowa, oowa, oo-oo-oo."

Regan stepped back to the wall and placed one leg on the top barre, sliding into a deep straddle split. As she relaxed into the pleasant burning sensation of her lengthening muscles, she heard a tap on the observation window. A girl stood outside, pulling her mouth wide open, sticking out her tongue, and crossing her eyes.

Regan crossed her own eyes. Lifting her leg off the barre, she silently mouthed, "Mel, you're crazy," and motioned her into the studio.

"We're on a break," Regan said after Mel entered.

Mel tucked her soccer ball under one arm and stepped over a girl sewing elastic onto a ballet slipper. "I figured that." She cocked her head toward the group around the boom box. "Cynthia and her natives are a tad more restless than Mrs. Vigil usually allows."

Regan glanced at the four girls, who were springing into the air as far as they could without bending their knees, sometimes veering off to the right and left like misguided rockets.

"What's the problem, Mel?" Regan launched herself straight-kneed into the air and bounced up and down. "You don't think this is normal behavior?"

They both laughed. "Actually, it's kind of hard to do." Regan rubbed her knee. "What's up?"

"Mom couldn't get me right after practice, so I walked over. She'll pick me up here."

"Perfect. I have something to show you. Rehearsal shouldn't be much longer . . ."

"No, Susan, do it this way." Cynthia's voice carried across the room.

"Now go right, then left, and . . . hey!" Cynthia and Susan collided in midair, then melted into a giggling heap on the floor.

Mel sat on her soccer ball. "How *do* you concentrate with all their noise?"

"I pretty much tuned them out years ago." Regan pulled her elbows into her waist, spread her fingers, and began swinging both her forearms sharply from right to left. "But, you know, when they do stop," she said, adding the footwork—swiveling on the balls of her feet with knees bent, "it's kind of like when the power goes out and you notice how noisy the fridge really is."

"That's a rosy way to look at it."

Mrs. Vigil entered the studio. "Okay, ladies, back to work." She looked at Mel. "Well, well, well—I'm pleased to see you've taken up dance again, Mel."

Mel grinned. "Not a chance, Mrs. Vigil."

"As soon as I invent soccer-dance, you'll be first to sign up?"

"Yes, ma'am—but until then, I'll be an 'appreciator.'" Mel went to sit in the waiting room.

"Let's go over Hand Jive before calling it a night," Mrs. Vigil said. "I want to see if everyone has that footwork." She swiveled partway through the step, pausing to look at Cynthia's group. "We're moving on now, Karaoke Quartet."

Cynthia stopped bouncing to her music and turned around to face Mrs. Vigil. "Sure thing, Mrs. V."

While Mrs. Vigil completed the step, the four of them snuck in one more "Oowa, oowa, oo-oo-oo" before Cynthia pushed the stop button.

Regan adjusted her elastic knee brace and moved to the second line.

"Regan, if that knee is still hurting," Mrs. Vigil said, "you need to stay off it. There'll be other performances this month. September is always busy."

Regan shook her head. "It's fine—I'm just wearing it to be careful. I can dance next Saturday."

Mrs. Vigil said, "Let me know how it's doing as the week goes on."

Regan didn't exactly *lie* to Mrs. Vigil. She was wearing the knee brace to be careful, and she would dance the following Saturday. Because there was no way she'd miss dancing with the New Mexico Jazz Dance Ensemble.

Music from *Grease* sounded through the studio. Cynthia and Susan squeezed into the center of the first row—directly in front of Regan—as the ensemble began the opening step, touch, clap. They were moving into the double forearm circles when Regan felt, more than saw, Cynthia move in the wrong direction and giggle about it.

"Cynthia!" Mrs. Vigil yelled over the music. "One, two, three, kick left; back, two, three, brush right. Again, ladies, two, three, higher legs; back, two, three, smile!"

Then the chorus section of the song blared from the stereo: "Born to hand jive, baby!" Regan liked the simplicity of that part of the choreography—grouped in counts of two.

She slapped her thighs with her hands on counts one, two—clapped her hands on counts three, four—pulsed right hand over left on five, six—left hand over right on seven, eight, all the while jumping on the beat in tiny speedy bounces.

As the dancers hit the final pose of Hand Jive, on their toes with knees turned in together and heads tilted to the side, applause erupted from the waiting room. Mel was the one making most of the commotion.

Mrs. Vigil crisply clapped her hands. "Okay, people, it's obvious some of us still have some polishing to do." She looked at Cynthia. "But we're out of time tonight. So *practice* this weekend, then we have rehearsals Monday, Wednesday, and Friday nights.

"I want a perfect performance on Saturday. And don't forget the auditions at Desert Vista Saturday afternoon. It'll be a busy day. Good-bye, ladies."

Regan grabbed her dance bag and dashed from the studio.

"Come talk while I change," she said to Mel.

Mel followed Regan to the dressing room.

"What'd you think?" Regan asked.

Mel let out a low whistle. "Every time I watch you dance, I thank my lucky genuine-imitation-leather miniature soccer ball key chain that we talked my mom into letting me quit dance. You're just plain out getting good, Regan."

Regan paused. "Truth?"

"Would I speak otherwise? The stuff you're doing is really hard. I was already a clod back in third grade."

Regan opened her locker. "You're *not* a clod. If we'd just traded mothers, we would have been set. Mine always wanted me to dance for a year and then try other things. Yours had your costume picked out for opening night." She pulled the pink tie out of her ponytail and let her light brown hair fall to her shoulders.

After removing her leotard and tights, she slipped jeans over her long legs, and pulled on a pink T-shirt. "Let's go."

They sat on the sidewalk in front of the studio and waited for their rides. The Southwestern Academy of Dance, located on the edge of Albuquerque, overlooked the vast west mesa. Regan never minded waiting there, especially when the sun set. That night the horizon looked like a stage backdrop lit in a two-color wash of salmon pink and apricot orange.

Mel spoke. "Hey, you wanted to show me something."

"Yeah, hold on a minute." Regan pulled a piece of turquoise paper out of her dance bag. "Look at this." She thrust the flyer at Mel.

Mel read aloud:

"DESERT VISTA MIDDLE SCHOOL TELEVISION ANNOUNCES
AUDITIONS FOR THE HOST OF
HOMEROOM EXERCISE
We are looking for a seventh-grade student to organize
and lead an exercise and dance show for the seventh grade
on our closed-circuit television station.
WHEN: Saturday, September 9, 4:00 P.M.
WHERE: DVTV Studio
BE PREPARED: To do a jazz warm-up,
learn a jazz combination, and
perform a jazz combination of your own.
LOOK SHARP AND GOOD LUCK!!!"

"So this is the audition Mrs. Vigil was talking about," Mel said. "Sounds like the job has your name on it."

Regan felt her cheeks flush. "It would be great, wouldn't it?" She pulled the flyer out of Mel's fingers. "But I'd have to win first."

"That should be easy enough."

"Not that easy. Mrs. Vigil is the school sponsor for the show, and she's put up flyers everywhere. It's not like I'll be the only one auditioning."

"Don't worry. You'll be great. You always make up the best dances," Mel said. "Except you're still wearing that brace I loaned you. How's your knee?"

"Most of the time it's okay," Regan said. "It didn't bother me much tonight. Hey, there's Mom. Got to go." She placed the flyer back into her bag. "Sure your mom's coming?"

Mel answered, "She'll be here."

Regan hurried toward the car.

"Don't forget!" Mel called. "Your house tomorrow night. We can work on your dance if you want."

"That would be great." Regan waved. "See you at five." She opened the car door and slid into the seat, careful not to bump her knee.

Chapter Two

Late the next afternoon, Regan watched over her father's shoulder. "Is that what's wrong?"

"Should be. Simple problem. It just took me a while to find the wire." Steven Shaffer reached beside the footlights and picked up a tool from the garage floor. "Here, you can fix it yourself."

Regan squatted down next to a double row of red, green, and blue outdoor floodlights. They were mounted inside a rectangular box open on one side.

"Take the wire stripper and pull about an inch of plastic coating off the wire. Then do it with this other wire."

She did.

"Now," he continued, "put the two wires inside this wire nut and twist. There. Let's see if that does it."

Regan pushed a button on the dimmer box and the lights splashed dazzling color on the stage at the back of the garage.

"We did it!" She leaped onto the stage, which thudded under her weight.

Regan curtsied to her father. "Thank you, stagehand, for the help with the footlights. Once the rip in the curtain is fixed, Le Grand Garage Théâtre will be good as new."

Her father reached out and tickled her until she curled up giggling. "Next weekend, Twinkle Toes— and you're helping."

"What's all the commotion?" Lana Shaffer appeared at the garage door.

"Just a dispute with the stage crew, Mom."

"You'd better be careful. A performer is *nothing* without a good crew." Mrs. Shaffer smiled at them. "I never imagined that this stage would still be here two years later. You know I don't mind losing the space." She sat on the edge of the stage. "But I thought you'd make it into an art studio, and then maybe a science lab."

"I like it just the way it is, Mom."

Mrs. Shaffer kissed Regan's cheek. "Dad and I have chores inside."

"I'm going to stay out here awhile."

"Don't forget to turn off the lights and unplug them when you're finished," Regan's dad said.

Regan watched them go to the kitchen. She gently stroked her left knee, then stood up and walked in a small circle around the stage.

During fifth grade, Regan and Mel would put on shows in the Shaffers' living room, but when they kept kicking furniture, Mrs. Shaffer relocated them to the garage and suggested building the stage. Simple plywood on the floor turned into a raised stage with lights and curtains. Now it was Le Grand Garage Théâtre.

Regan lowered the garage door. Darkness closed in and she stepped back on the stage into the brightness. Humming the "Waltz of the Flowers" from the *Nutcracker,* Regan brushed her feet into waltz turns, twirling and stretching into arabesques—wrapped in darkness and light, feeling complete in her solitude.

She waltzed to the front of the stage and scooped up her dance journal as if it were a bouquet of flowers tossed by an admirer. On the cover was an ink drawing of a dancer in second arabesque, with just a touch of pink pastel smudging the romantic-length tutu and gardenia at the nape of her neck.

Last year in Regan's Lang/Lit class, the teacher had them start a journal. Everyone wrote about everyday things that happened—what classes they took, who liked whom, what movies they saw.

Regan had started that way, but soon found she preferred writing about dance. She traded her notebook for a special journal that had a shadowy sketch of a dancer and a quote about dance on each page.

In the warm glow of the footlights, she opened her journal to the first page. The quote read:

> We are all dancers. We use movement to express ourselves—our hungers, pains, angers, joys, confusions, fears—long before we use words, and we understand the meanings of movements long before we understand those of words.
>
> —Franklin Stevens

Under the quote Regan had written:

> I think Franklin Stevens is very smart. I wish more people understood this about themselves.
>
> Anyway, this was the best day of my life!!! We finally, finally, finally started on pointe today! Mrs. Vigil showed us how to soften the hard sole and toe of our shoes with our hands, how to work the lamb's-wool pad, and how to tie the beeeautifulll pink ribbons. She only let us walk on half-pointe around the room. But once, when she wasn't looking, I went all the way up on top of my toes! It was like rising into the heavens!

Most of the students had stopped their journals after school ended that year, but Regan had continued hers. She flipped through the journal to find the current page.

Dancing teaches you a sense of accomplishment. The discipline of dance teaches you self-discipline. You know you can achieve what you set out to do, not just with dance, but with anything you choose.

—Melissa Hayden

Regan took out her pen and began writing:

> **Dance can help me achieve anything I choose, Miss Hayden? I hope you're right. Because there seem to be better and better dancers around the older I get. More competition. Am I really as good as Mel says I am?**

At the bottom of the page, Regan drew a large question mark in tiny hearts.

"Regan . . . Regan?" The door from the kitchen stood open.

"Hey, Twinkle Toes, we've been calling," her dad said. "Won't Mel be here soon?"

"You're right, Dad, thanks. Be right in." Mel would help her sift through what she'd choreographed that morning. Mel had a good eye for what was on and what was off.

She closed her journal, stepped off the stage, turned on the overhead lights, and squinted in the harsh fluorescent glare. The magic was broken—until next time.

Chapter Three

A half hour later, Regan sat at her desk. She nudged a pewter fairy that hung from the bottom of her bulletin board and sent it spinning in circles. The fairy hovered in the air holding a faceted crystal ball in its right hand. The crystal caught the evening sun shining through the window. Red, yellow, green, and violet rainbows jittered in patterns over Mel as she sat on Regan's bed. "Okay, what's the plan?"

"I've got the combo mostly worked out—but there're just some places . . ." Regan touched the fairy and stopped the rainbows. She looked at Mel. "You know, you are the *best* for helping."

"Just part of my job description. Let's see what you've got."

"I thought of going with hip-hop, but decided to stay with jazz. So first I want to show you this video and check out the style." Regan pulled several magazines out of a drawer before coming to the video.

"*YM*?" Mel said. She picked up the magazine and flipped through its pages. "You're not actually *reading* this, are you?"

Regan shrugged. "The articles are kind of fun." She sat on the floor with her back to the bed and opened her legs into a split. She plopped the magazine in front of her and began reading. "'Hot Looks You Don't Have to Buy at a Store,' 'How to Find Jeans That Fit'—you could use that one, Mel . . ."

Mel pushed Regan's shoulder. "Thanks loads."

"Okay, so those don't do anything for you. Here's something that's kind of cute." Regan got up and placed the magazine on her desk.

Taking a long-sleeved shirt off a hanger, she looked back at the magazine. Then she unzipped her jeans and kicked her way out of them while she read the directions in the article. She buttoned the bottom two buttons of the shirt, stepped into it, and raised the collar to her waist.

Mel stared at Regan. "What *are* you doing?"

"I'm going to make this shirt into a skirt." Regan tied the sleeves into a double knot at her waist, and then buttoned the rest of the buttons. She put her hands on her hips, asking, "Well, what do you think?"

"I think I'll stick to my sweats—no pun intended."

Regan laughed. "*Naaaw,*" she said. "I think they missed on this one, but some of the other how-to articles might be good."

"Oh, great," Mel teased, "another source for how-to articles. It's not like you don't already have a gazillion how-to books."

"I'm not that bad, smarty." Regan hung the shirt back in the closet. "I only have one shelf of how-tos, and they're about a lot of different things. My mom has a complete bookcase just for books about how to raise kids—and she only has one of those."

Mel cleared her throat. "Like mother, like—"

"Don't say it." Regan finished zipping her jeans back up. "Now that you mention it, I better take another look at that book about how to be successful at dance auditions."

Regan's bedroom door swung open and banged against the wall. "Oops. Hi, Regan, hi, Mel. What are you guys up to?"

"Aaah . . . hi, Becky," Regan said.

"Mom had me bike over with some church stuff for your mom, Regan."

Becky sat down on the desk. "Are you guys reading? I thought you'd be practicing for the audition."

"We were just—"

"Look at this ad." Becky held up a page to Regan. "My mom told me your mom was going to take you to the dermatologist because you're getting zits. If you used this cream, you might not need to go."

Regan sunk down on the bed next to Mel.

"Well, I—" Regan started.

"Regan, did you hear Cynthia and Susan are auditioning? You're auditioning, aren't you?"

"Yes, I'm really—"

"Cynthia and Susan are pretty good. But you're good, too, right? Say, got to go. Mom said to come right back. So bye." Becky twittled her fingers in a wave. "See you guys later, bye." Becky walked out the door.

Regan sat staring at the open door.

"She is the *strangest* girl," Mel said. "I'm surprised she doesn't hyperventilate and keel right over."

"She has always babbled like that. I'll never forget what she said to you in third grade when you had just moved to town. 'Are you a boy or a girl? The teacher said your name is really Melanie, but you want to be called Mel. Why would you want that?'"

"How can you remember that?"

"Because it made me so mad, that's why."

Mel ran her hand up the back of her razored short hair. "It was the hair that confused her."

"Yeah, well, she could have kept it to herself."

Mel stood and dramatically spoke. "And how 'for-tu-a-tuss' the teacher had the wisdom to put me in the desk next to you. My growth surely would have been stunted under a lesser influence." Mel bowed with a flourish.

Regan shoved Mel's butt with her foot.

"Hey, that's the last time I bow to you!"

"Next time, try bowing to me instead of away from me with your derriere in my face."

They were still laughing when Regan's mom entered with an armload of laundry. "Pretty giggly choreography session, isn't it, girls?"

"*We* don't giggle," Mel said, straight-faced. "We guffaw!"

That started them again.

"Whatever you call it," Mrs. Shaffer said, chuckling, "dinner will be ready in about an hour."

Mel put her arm around Mrs. Shaffer's shoulders. "Thanks, Other Mom."

"My pleasure, Other Daughter."

"Do you want help, Mom?" Regan asked.

"No—work on your dance," Mrs. Shaffer called as she left the room. "Becky tells me Cynthia and Susan are auditioning, too."

Regan stopped laughing.

"So what?" Mel said. "They weren't that good when I took class, and it takes a klutz to know a klutz." Mel pulled her lucky soccer ball key chain out of her pocket and twirled it in a circle. "I didn't pay that much attention to their dancing yesterday at rehearsal, but they didn't seem so great."

"Well, they're better dancers than you remember," Regan replied. "You never know about Cynthia—sometimes she's on, sometimes off. Depends on how much she wants something."

"You've got nothing to worry about," Mel said. "But if you want, I'll loan you my lucky genuine-imitation-leather miniature soccer ball key chain."

"Thanks, but the only thing that will help me is a good dance." Regan put a videotape into the VCR. "Watch and tell me what you think."

The dancers on the screen turned, jumped, and slid through a complicated routine. Regan danced parts of the steps with the video. Slide, spin high spin low, out out, shoulder roll, head right, jump land. She stopped the video. "See, I changed most of it, like the spin, and I think the head looks cool after the shoulder. The carpet caught my feet on the spin, but what do you think?"

"Do it again. Your version."

Regan danced. Slide, spin high spin low, out out, shoulder roll, head right, jump land, knee buckle— "Ouch," she said softly. A pain stabbed through her knee, then vanished. She hopped on her right foot and grabbed hold of the bookshelf.

Mel jumped up and stood beside her in an instant. "Whoa—are you all right? Your knee again?"

"No, uh, it was probably just the carpet." Regan turned away from Mel and wiped at her eyes. How was she going to beat Cynthia at the audition if her knee crashed on her like that? "This is a terrible place to practice. We should be using the stage in the garage."

"All the same. Sit down a minute."

Regan moved to the bed. Her knee worked fine, but it felt sore. "Maybe—I should put ice on it, just to be on the safe side. Could you get some in a kitchen towel?"

Mel reached for the doorknob. "Sure thing."

"Don't let Mom or Dad see you."

"Don't worry." Mel left the room.

Regan leaned back on the bed. She should have put the knee brace on. She'd been doing fine with the brace. So what if she needed to wear it during the audition? Mrs. Vigil wouldn't think anything of it.

Chapter Four

At the television studio, Regan stretched over the length of her legs. She yawned. She'd gotten up early that morning for the jazz ensemble's show at the mall. Her knee had been fine and the energy between the dancers and audience electrifying.

Regan studied the others trying out for the show. She knew most of the kids—at least half of them danced at Southwestern. But no sign of Cynthia or Susan. Maybe they had changed their minds. Probably not—they were always late.

There was no sign of Mel, either.

Regan stood up, found a chair to use as a ballet barre, and began warming up.

She lowered her body into a grand plié and looked around the room. It seemed almost like a real TV studio, not just a large classroom. Backdrops hid blackboards, and heavy black paper covered the tall windows. The room excited Regan with its cameras, lights, and sets. The show's host would need to be clever to fit workout combinations in such a tiny space.

Regan was running in place, shaking pre-audition jitters out of her hands, when she heard a commotion by the door.

"Hey, Cynthia, Susan, which one of you is going to win?" a guy fiddling with a camera called out.

"We haven't decided yet." Cynthia giggled.

Susan echoed, "Yeah, we haven't decided yet."

"But definitely," Cynthia said confidently, "we need a name change. *Homeroom Exercise*—yuck."

Cynthia took off her warm-up outfit, wadded it up, and threw it in the corner. She wore black thong-backed dance trunks over a red leotard with a black thunderbolt across the chest. It was the outfit Regan had seen advertised in *Dance Magazine* and wanted to buy.

A familiar voice whispered into her ear, "Are you ready to knock 'em dead?"

She turned to find Mel. "I was starting to wonder if you were coming."

"Wouldn't miss it. Here, rub the key chain for good luck. I never play a game without it."

Regan gladly rubbed the imitation leather, but all she really needed was Mel there.

Handing the key chain back, she tilted over the chair in an arabesque stretch. At that moment Cynthia passed by, calling to Susan, "Hey, toss me my brush." Cynthia reached out for her brush and knocked Regan with her hip, almost tipping her off balance.

"Whoa," Regan and Mel said at the same time.

"Not that one, Susan, the vent brush." Cynthia breezed on. "That hair clip, too."

Mel said, "Is she just clumsy and ill-mannered, or are we invisible?"

"Whichever's the case, I'd better rub that key chain again for safety's sake."

Mrs. Vigil's voice stopped them from continuing. "It's time, dancers."

Mel gave Regan a thumbs-up.

"Line up to get your audition numbers, and pin them to the front of your leotards," Mrs. Vigil instructed.

Cynthia and Susan darted to the front of the line to be first. They didn't know what Regan's book *How to Audition* said—that the later you dance in an audition, the more memorable you are to the judges. Regan lined up almost last, attaching the number sixteen to her powder blue leotard.

"Dancers," Mrs. Vigil called, "to the center of the room, please."

Mrs. Vigil hung her sweater on the back of a chair. Regan took both ballet and jazz classes from her and loved them. If Regan got the host position, she'd get to work with Mrs. Vigil even more.

Two other teachers, along with Mrs. Vigil, would choose the host, but they sat in the front, and Mrs. Vigil led the warm-up and combination.

"Walk through it with me one more time." Mrs. Vigil faced front. "Step, kick ball change, kick ball change, head toss toss, feet together. Hop hop, cross ball change, spin spin, land. Hitch kick, body roll, and out and out and out. Hop hop, jump turn, run slide split. Questions?" Mrs. Vigil nimbly got to her feet faster than most of the students.

"Would you do it one more time?" Cynthia asked.

"Not the whole combination, Cynthia," Mrs. Vigil replied. "But I'll answer specific questions. The host of this show needs to be a quick study."

"How many hops before the cross ball change?" one girl asked.

"Two."

One of the three guys auditioning called out, "Mrs. Vigil, did you want a full body roll up to relevé, or just stay flat?"

"Stay flat, or you can't get into the following step. Anything else?" asked the teacher. No one spoke. "Take about five minutes to go over it, and then we'll do it in groups and start narrowing this down." Mrs. Vigil joined the other teachers and started whispering to them.

"Cynthia, how did this part go?" Susan asked.

"Like this." Cynthia moved through the first part with the head roll. She reversed a couple of steps, so it didn't work out right.

Regan thought of helping Susan, as she would in a class, but this was different. And Susan probably wouldn't accept her help anyway. Well—maybe Susan would take her help, but only if Cynthia allowed it.

Mrs. Vigil sharply clapped her hands two times. "Let's have numbers one through ten center, please."

Cynthia and Susan lined up with the first group. Susan was a little shaky, but Cynthia pulled it off, even with mistakes. She had great stage presence, which always made up for her technique errors.

Mrs. Vigil called the second half of the dancers. Step, kick ball change, kick ball change, head toss toss, feet together. Hop hop, cross ball change, and on to the end. The short combination appeared to stop as soon as it began.

Mel tugged at her elbow. "Way to go, champ!"

Regan smiled.

"Okay, dancers," Mrs. Vigil said as she stood up. "This is a hard decision, but we must make the first cut. Thank you all for trying out. Everyone danced beautifully." Mrs. Vigil paused before continuing. "If I call your number, please come to the center of the room and stay for the second half of the audition. Numbers one, two, seven, and sixteen. Thank you, everyone."

Regan let out a puff of air. Cynthia and Susan, a girl named Ann, and Regan moved out to the middle of the room.

"Congratulations," Regan said to the other three.

Ann smiled and said thanks.

Cynthia nodded curtly. "You, too," she said, as she turned to talk to Susan. "Now, what did we put after the stag leap in the combination?"

"Dancers, your own jazz combinations are the last part of the audition. We'll go in order of your numbers."

Cynthia stopped talking to listen to Mrs. Vigil a moment, then suddenly turned to Regan. "So, Regan, just how bad is your knee, anyway? I see you're still wearing a brace."

Regan froze.

Mel held up her lucky genuine-imitation-leather miniature soccer ball key chain. Regan's moment of panic melted away. She really wanted the host position. Calm—she just needed to be calm.

"You're up first, Cynthia," Mrs. Vigil announced.

Regan automatically began to critique Cynthia's dance. She looked good, even though her dance was a hodgepodge.

Susan was next. Her dance looked like Cynthia's except in reverse, and with a few more mistakes.

Ann performed third. Though she made a real effort, her piece was not as good as Cynthia's or Susan's.

Finally, it was Regan's turn. She licked her dry lips and shook her hands. Time to focus. When the music started, her uncertainty disappeared. She exploded—dance—no other thrill could measure up.

She finished her combination with a dazzling double spin into a layout down to her knee. The students watching burst into applause. Mel jumped around the room, cheering.

"Everybody, everybody," Mrs. Vigil called out. "Wonderful dances, girls. We will make our decision and announce it Tuesday morning during homeroom, since Monday is an in-service day. Thank you all, again."

Mel leaped onto Regan's back. "You've won! You choreographer extraordinaire! You've won!"

"Hold on. Not so fast." Regan disentangled herself from Mel. "Don't underestimate the power of Cynthia's stage presence. Who knows what the judges think?"

"I know what they think," Mel declared loudly, snapping gum in her mouth. "That you're the host of *Homeroom Exercise.*"

Chapter Five

Monday night, after her ballet class at the academy, Regan sewed ribbons onto a new pair of pointe shoes. It had taken eight months for her first pair to wear out. Regan had been elated when the shiny pink satin finally tore on the toes. Then it looked like she was getting somewhere.

After that first pair, her shoes had broken down more rapidly. They were spending more time on pointe and learning variations from the classical ballets. That night Mrs. Vigil had taught the opening to the Gold Fairy Variation from *Sleeping Beauty*.

Regan put the new shoes carefully in her bag, then picked up the old ones, knotting all four ribbons together at the ends. She then hung them, opposite her first pair, from the corner of her bookshelf.

She walked on half-pointe around her room, reviewing the first step of the variation. She lifted her torso and opened her arms into second position—feeling regal and courtly. Grand battement, passé, glide forward–and then again on the left.

When she mastered the Gold Fairy Variation, she would buy herself the fairy ornament with wings tipped in gold that she had seen in a catalog.

Regan stretched her neck and back. It was odd that she felt so tired—no school that day and only one ballet class that night. She peeled off her tights to look at her knee. The skin felt warm and looked red around the kneecap. She poked at the red area. Was it a little swollen or just her imagination?

Regan changed into leggings and then pulled out of her dance bag a package of frozen peas she had smuggled from the freezer. She wrapped the cold package over the top of her left knee and lay back on her bed. She couldn't recall hitting her knee on anything, twisting it while dancing, or—or anything at all she had done to it.

It didn't hurt her all the time, but the problem had been hanging on for at least a month now. She should probably tell her parents, but if she did, they might make her take a break from dance classes. Then what about *Homeroom Exercise*?

Not that she had that to worry about. She didn't even know if she would win—Cynthia was good. But she still hoped she had a chance. The waiting made her crazy.

Regan reached for her journal and opened it to a page where she'd followed instructions from an article in *Jump* magazine, "Goals: With Planning You Can Achieve."

Young dancers are like leaves—blow on them, and they move.

—Sir Frederic Ashton

Here were her goals:

Career in Dance

1. Professional Ballet Dancer
   a. learn all the classical variations on pointe
   b. audition and be accepted for a summer dance camp
   c. convince Mom and Dad to send me to a fine arts high school back east
   d. audition and be accepted to a major ballet company
2. Professional Dancer in Music Videos
   a. win a jazz choreography contest in Dance Magazine
   b. move with Mom and Dad to Los Angeles during high school and start going on open audition calls for jazz dancers

**c. get to know and be hired by a major
rock star for her/his video**

Looking at the list again, Regan realized she had a problem with her 1c. She'd miss her parents too much to go. Or maybe they'd miss her too much.

Regan scratched out 1c and replaced it with:

c. win host position on <u>Homeroom Exercise</u>

That goal felt better.

Regan put her journal on the bed and the drippy pea bag on a stack of Kleenex. She checked her knee— good, no swelling.

She untwined her French braid until her hair hung loose. When she was little, her mother said it was the color of brown sugar. She had tasted it and was surprised to find nothing sweet about a mouthful of hair.

She sat at her dressing table and looked into the mirror. Was *Jump* magazine right? She'd worked on the plans, but did that really mean you'd achieve your goals?

Well, tomorrow she'd find out about 1c.

Chapter Six

Regan's heels jittered a steady rhythm and her hands danced across her desk. Pas de bourrée, pas de bourrée, over and over they tiptoed, until Mel slid into the seat in front of her.

"How's the host of *Homeroom Exercise* this morning?"

"Shhh—don't jinx it."

"Regan, Regan, it's the big day—it's here!" Becky came down the aisle toward her, knocking a book off a desk. "Who do you think won? People said you were good Saturday, but are you better than Cynthia? What do you think?" The bell rang. "Oops, I'd better sit down."

Regan felt sick.

Then Cynthia and Susan arrived together and sat at their desks. A cluster of girls twisted around in their seats to face Cynthia. They looked like the swans surrounding Odette in the ballet *Swan Lake*. Only these swans wore short dresses with taupe-colored stockings and platform shoes.

"Awesome dancing Saturday!" one girl bubbled. Cynthia and Susan's group of friends agreed loudly until the teacher told them to face front for the morning announcements.

This is it, Regan thought.

"Good morning, students," the voice of the vice-principal said. "Remember to buy Stick Up for Earth stickers in the cafeteria during lunch. The student council is selling them for two dollars. The money is going to the Save the Whales campaign. There are still Desert Vista Diamondback T-shirts available in the school store. Show your school pride and buy one today."

The voice from the speaker on the wall went on and on. Regan started to think they weren't going to announce the winner when her attention snapped back to the voice.

"And last this morning, I have the name of the winner of the seventh-grade contest for the host of the new DVTV—Desert Vista Television, that is—show called *Homeroom Exercise*. The thirty-minute show to be aired on Friday mornings will begin this Friday."

Regan held her breath.

The vice-principal continued, "Your host for the new show will beeeee—Regan Shaffer!"

"Yessss!" Regan exhaled.

The voice continued, "Congratulations, Regan. Have a good day, students."

"All right, Regan," Mel yelled. Mel, Becky, and most of the class cheered as the bell rang to go to first period.

Regan felt as if a warm light radiated through her body. It happened. She won. She did it.

Mel dragged Regan out of her seat, and they slowly made their way toward the door amid high fives and congratulations—except around Cynthia. Cynthia sat unmoving at her desk.

Regan felt she had to say something. She stopped. "Cynthia, you really *did* dance well."

"I did, didn't I? Although the judges obviously thought I had an off day, and you were the lucky one."

Cynthia slowly rose from her seat—not taking her eyes off Regan. Surrounded by her friends, Cynthia left the room.

Mel broke the eerie silence. "Do the words *drama queen* come to mind?"

A laugh escaped from Regan. "Actually, I was thinking more in the line of the daughter of an evil sorcerer—like in *Swan Lake*."

"That will do," Mel said. "But—moving right along, *you* are the host of *Homeroom Exercise*."

Mel and Regan danced down the hallway to their next class, bellowing, "There's no business like show business."

Regan had awakened many times during the night, certain it was morning, only when she opened her eyes, it was still dark.

But this time, when she awoke, morning had finally arrived. Time for *Homeroom Exercise*.

Regan leaped out of bed and into the opening routine for the show. Bend, bend, bend, stretch up. Twist, twist, twist, stretch up. She felt stiff and achy. She'd had only three days to put the first show together—she must have overdone it. She headed for the shower—she couldn't wait to get to the DVTV studio.

An hour later, Regan walked into the studio. The stage lights glared, the music blasted from the tape player, and the camera operators were behind their cameras.

Mrs. Vigil greeted her. "Good morning. Are you ready to make these kids break a sweat?"

"I think that's going to be quite a trick with some of the girls not wanting their makeup to run."

"Your choreography will be compelling enough to

get even the most sedentary of our students off their backsides. Anyway, participation is part of everyone's homeroom grade."

They both laughed.

Mrs. Vigil pointed to Regan's knee. "How's the knee this morning? Good and warmed up? The show starts in ten minutes."

"It's fine, and I'm ready to go." Regan took off her knee brace, finished adjusting her black leg warmers over her jazz shoes, and stood in the center of the set. She walked through the jazz routine for the second half of the show. It worked perfectly in the small space of the studio, and the kids could do it in their rooms with the desks pushed back.

Jeff, a camera operator, called out, "One minute to air, Regan."

Just as she and Jeff had practiced the last three days, Regan took her place. The music started and she began. Bend, bend, bend, stretch up. Twist, twist, twist, stretch up. She continued the pattern during the introduction by one of the off-camera crew.

"Gooood morning to you from DVTV, Desert Vista Television. Get up out of your chairs, push 'em back, and welcome the host of *Homeroom Exercise*—Regan Shaffer." A soundtrack of applause played over the music.

Regan opened her mouth to say good morning as she normally would and surprised herself with a DJ sound. "Good morning, you crazies out there. Let's make some noise and rattle the windows because it's *Homeroom Exercise* time. Just follow along—you, too, teachers!" Jeff gave Regan the thumbs-up sign. She smiled and continued, "Now step touch, step touch, side together side, step touch, step touch, side together side."

Regan moved them through the ten-minute warm-up and then into the low-impact aerobics. She continued that pace for the next ten minutes. But once their hearts were pumping, she started the jazz combination. "Let's get you all fine-tuned for the Winter Dance. Instead of just hanging out by the gym wall, try these moves. They'll blow the teachers away but not get you in-school suspension. Now reach high then low, hip circle, pivot around; shoulder, two, three, bounce; shoulder, two, three, bounce . . ."

After repeating the combination several times, she moved into the cooldown. Sweat poured down her back—nothing had come close to what she was feeling at that moment. She was supercharged and floating higher than ever before.

The show came to a close. She waved both her hands at the camera. "See ya next time, you crazies. This is *Homeroom Exercise* with Regan Shaffer!"

Jeff made a slicing motion with his hand across his throat. "Weeee're out!"

The crew clapped and whistled. Mrs. Vigil flew to Regan's side. "What a show! I know you're a great dancer, but I had no idea what a performer you are!"

A counselor came through the door. "They were *all* dancing—every person in every seventh-grade classroom. The principal was a little concerned about the noise level, though. The other grades just may have to participate, too!"

Regan hugged Mrs. Vigil. "Thank you, thank you, thank you for choosing me!"

She rushed out of the studio to change. Once in the empty bathroom, she whooped and hollered. She leaned over the sink a moment, holding a cool paper towel to the back of her neck. She had to get to first-period math.

In the hallway, students mobbed Regan with congratulations. When Mel got to her, she was ecstatic. "You were great! Everybody loved the workout. Even the guys did almost everything. And just where did you get that DJ-sounding patter? I've never heard you talk like that."

Regan pulled Mel to the side of the hall. "I don't know what happened to me. Something inside me, someone different, took over. My glittery ballet fairy, I usually feel guiding me when I dance, wasn't there. Instead there was something powerful pushing me to say those things."

Mel looked at Regan. "What goes on with you astonishes me, Regan."

"It's weird, isn't it?"

"Not weird, just different. You're just different. In a good way," Mel added quickly.

"Aren't we both different like that in the same way?" Regan asked.

"Not exactly," Mel disagreed. "What you just described doesn't happen to me when I'm scoring in a game. That's something special you have. Where we *are* both the same is in knowing what we want," Mel stated. "And that's different from the other kids."

Before Regan could answer, the boy who sat behind her in homeroom flipped at the side of her hair as he passed her. "Sure was better than what we normally do in homeroom. Not a bad-looking little outfit, either, Regan."

A wolf whistle rang through the hall, followed by, "Way to go, Shaffer!" A bunch of seventh-grade boys shuffled by the two girls. Regan blushed.

A girl named Tammy came running toward her. "Regan! You're a celebrity! Can I have your autograph? Everybody in the whole seventh grade is talking about your show."

"You're a hit," Mel said proudly.

Regan linked arms with Mel. "This is so strange. People who have never spoken to me are yelling compliments to me in the hall. Is this what it's like to be a celebrity?"

"I guess so," Mel said. "And you know people say celebrities are a little different—so you'll fit right in."

"Ha, ha, funny girl," replied Regan.

"You now belong to the people, my dear, and I'll be your agent," Mel said with a bow. "But first, may I have your autograph, Madame Celebrity?"

Chapter Seven

Regan settled down to study. Since the show had started, she'd learned to follow a strict schedule in order to get everything done. That night, after homework, she still had routines to work on for Friday's show.

She had also found that as the host of *Homeroom Exercise* she'd acquired all kinds of new friends with no effort on her part. People she didn't know waved to her, gave her cuts in line, and one day a cute guy gave her a slice of pizza at lunch. Most of them had never cared much about her before. It wasn't that she didn't know anyone other than Mel—but she wasn't exactly well known, either. Now they were acting like Regan was one of them.

But her newfound fame would be short-lived if she didn't keep up her grades; she needed to study. She cleared a stool next to her desk, then propped up her leg. Both of her knees ached that night, but the left knee was actually swollen. Oh, well, it would go away. It had before.

Regan worked her way through ten math problems and a social studies chapter. All she had left was that night's "Write Away" paragraph for Lang/Lit. Then she could spend a little time on the show. She read the assignment. "Which of the following three childhood rhymes best describes your life at this moment and why: 'Humpty Dumpty'; 'Row, Row, Row Your Boat'; or 'Little Miss Muffet.'" Regan cracked up. She wondered if her teacher got the topics out of a book or made them up. As she scanned the rhymes, she sang, "Row, row, row your boat, gently down the stream; merrily, merrily, merrily, merrily; life is but a dream."

She turned on the computer. Life is but a dream. Did that mean, life is so wonderful it's like a dream, or life isn't real, it's only a dream? She clicked on an icon and shifted her leg. Her knee just wasn't right. She reached over to take a look when her father walked in.

"Good night, Regan." Her dad looked over her shoulder and picked up a newspaper she had on her desk. "Are you writing about the literary merit of newspaper advertising?"

"Not quite, but they do have us writing about rhymes." Regan smiled up at her father. "Take a look at that ad," she said. "It's a fuchsia and it looks just like a group of ballerinas. Don't you think so?"

Mr. Shaffer nodded. "It's also called a ballerina plant."

"Then it's definitely perfect for my room."

"Regan, with all you're doing, you don't have time to care for a plant. The last two in your room died."

"I'll water this one."

"A fuchsia needs more than just water. It won't flower like the one in this picture without the perfect light, fertilizer, and proper watering."

Regan touched her knee. It felt bigger than before.

"Just give it more thought before you decide. Don't stay up too late." He leaned over to give her a kiss on the head. "What's with the knee rubbing?"

"Oh, nothing." Her robe slid off her knee.

"What's this?" Her dad squatted beside her. "Your knee's as big as a grapefruit. When did this happen?"

"No wonder it hurts," Regan said, looking at her knee. "I had no idea—it got like this while I was studying."

"Lana!" Regan's father called, "Lana, come look at Regan's knee."

Her mother came in. "Oh, my word. Did you twist it in ballet class this afternoon?"

"No, I didn't. It's been giving me trouble for about a month, but it's never done this."

"*A month!*" Mrs. Shaffer looked up from Regan's knee. "Why didn't you tell me?"

"It wasn't a big deal. The aches would come and go. I'd forget all about it." She looked at her mom. "But this time it hurts."

Her mom stood up. "Let's get ice on it and call the doctor's service—see what they say."

Regan stared at her knee. It looked like the knee of a giraffe—grossly out of proportion to the rest of her leg.

By late the next morning, Regan sat in the office of an orthopedic specialist. The white paper protecting the table rustled loudly as Regan adjusted her weight from one hip to the other—then, complete quiet.

Regan's mother broke the silence. "I still don't understand why you didn't tell me about your knee. We could have done something before it got this bad."

"It didn't seem important."

"Not important! Look at it."

"I didn't mean important—it's just that it didn't seem like a problem before last night. I'm sorry, Mom."

The room was quiet again. They waited.

Regan stroked her forehead under her bangs. What a waste of time. It was just a sprain. The swelling had gone down some, and it didn't hurt as much. She didn't see why Dr. Wills had made such a big deal out of it and sent her to this other doctor.

Without warning, the door swung open. Regan stared into the chest of a tall man in a white coat with his head bent over a clipboard. The bright lights of the room glared off his bald head.

"So. Uhm-hum." Still looking at the papers in his hand, the man stepped back and blindly squatted onto a small round stool with three wheels.

Regan pictured him missing the stool and falling on his butt. She suppressed a giggle.

"Uhm-hum." The man cleared his throat, then, without taking his eyes from the chart, spoke. "I'm Dr. Kruel."

Mrs. Shaffer, sitting in a chair next to the exam table, gently patted Regan's thigh. "Our pediatrician, Dr. Wills, sent us over to have you look at my daughter's knee."

"Yes, I know." Dr. Kruel reached his long legs out in front of his body, planted his heels on the floor, and pulled the stool and himself to the exam table.

His cold hands surrounded Regan's swollen knee just below her rolled-up shorts. She shivered.

"Pain here?" Dr. Kruel pushed on the outside of her knee. All the puffiness moved toward the inside of her knee like soft Jell-O sloshing to the side of a bowl.

"Gag—how gross. What's in there?" Regan wrinkled up her face.

"Does it hurt?" the doctor repeated.

"Not really—not like last night."

Regan's mother spoke. "This swelling is so odd, doctor. It came on quite suddenly."

The doctor bent Regan's left leg back until her heel touched the back of her thigh. He rotated her lower leg to the right and then to the left, while feeling around the sides of her knee. "I'll need a fluid sample from the knee, an X ray, and blood tests before I can tell you anything."

"Fluid samples and blood tests? What for? What do you think it is?"

Regan heard the worry in her mom's voice.

"I won't get all the results back until sometime on Tuesday next week. Meanwhile, I don't want her on that leg. I want her on two aspirin every six hours. The nurse will fit her with a splint and crutches and set up the tests. I'll talk with you on Tuesday." And without another word Dr. Kruel opened the door and walked out.

"Sometime on Tuesday! But I'm dancing Friday morning. It's just a sprain. Can't we go back to Dr. W.? It'll be all right in a day or two."

"Regan, just calm down."

"Mom, nobody else knows the show. I've got to do it."

"You are given only one body in this lifetime and you have to listen to it." Mrs. Shaffer hugged her. "I know not dancing is difficult for you, but we've got to do this. Dr. Wills thinks it's important you see this specialist and follow his advice or she wouldn't have sent us here. Dr. Kruel is the expert. We need to see what he finds out."

Regan felt heavy.

After the full day of appointments and tests, Regan was exhausted by the time they got home that afternoon. She'd been feeling that way a lot lately.

"Hold on, Regan. I'll move the table."

"I used to think kids were having fun on crutches." Regan let her mother guide her onto the living room couch. She handed her mom the crutches and rubbed a sore spot under her arm. "Mom, could you get me some ice, please?"

"Sure, sweetie." Her mother headed for the kitchen.

Regan stared at her knee, wanting to see inside it.

Her mother returned with the ice.

"Thanks, Mom. I've *got* to get this swelling down before the show Friday."

"Regan," her mother said, "just stop. No dancing until the test results. We can't risk you hurting it further. And you need to tell Mrs. Vigil."

"Mrs. Vigil!" Regan adjusted the pillow behind her head. "This is so stupid. Don't you think this is overkill, Mom? I don't need this splint, and the swelling will be down by morning."

"It's not overkill," Regan's mother said. "Do you want to do something that will permanently injure you and keep you from the dancing career you want so much?" Her mother's hands trembled slightly as she released the Velcro straps to put the ice bag on Regan's knee. "You need to call Mrs. Vigil tonight or tell her tomorrow you can't dance on Friday."

Regan sat up on the couch. "Not yet, Mom, okay? If I tell her now she might replace me with someone else."

Lana Shaffer sat on the edge of the couch. "Regan, is that fair of you? How would you feel if you were the teacher, and Friday morning the host of the show comes hobbling in on crutches and you had to cancel at the last minute?"

Regan closed her eyes and sighed. But what if Mrs. Vigil let someone else do it and everyone liked that person better?

Chapter Eight

Thursday morning, Regan maneuvered her way into homeroom. She found moving down the aisle a challenge on crutches. Move the crutches a few inches, hop the right foot over a few inches, move the crutches, hop the foot, move, hop, crutch, foot.

Regan had made it to her desk and hopped around to aim her rear at the seat when Mel appeared. "I told you I'd come early to help. What time did you get here?" Mel took the crutches and leaned them against the wall.

"Early. I wanted to make sure I had plenty of time to get down the hall." Regan wiggled her backpack off her shoulders and then arranged her full, shin-length denim skirt down over most of the splint.

Mel got an extra chair to prop up Regan's leg and sat in front of her. "Well, this is creepy, Hop-a-long. I want to see the stuff in your knee mush back and forth."

"Sorry," Regan said. "You missed out. The swelling is practically all gone and it doesn't hurt. It feels so stupid wearing this splint. People will think I'm faking it, but Mom insisted."

"Did you call Mrs. Vigil last night?"

Regan looked down at her desk. "No—I—I just wasn't ready. Mel, if I tell her, she'll give it to someone else—probably Cynthia."

Regan felt her eyelids flutter. "Look, Mrs. Vigil already knows I've been having trouble with this knee, but that it hasn't kept me from dancing. I just have to be able to show her that this is temporary."

"Regan," Mel said suspiciously, "what are you planning? What do you mean—show her?"

"No big deal. The swelling's down. The pain's gone. I take the splint off long enough to see Mrs. Vigil after third period. Tell her I sprained my knee and could we please cancel the show for just this week. I'd be back on the job next week. She says yes, take care of yourself. I leave, put the splint back on, and no one's the wiser."

"Don't you think someone might mention to her you're wearing a splint?"

"No one's going to talk to her about it. Other than you, the kids who know me don't even have class with her. And no one's going to really notice anyway."

The door to the classroom banged open. Students trickled into the room in twos and threes. They spotted Regan's splint immediately.

"What happened to you?"

"Did you break it?"

"Nice-looking cast."

"Whoa—coming through!" Becky went sliding past the row of desks on Regan's crutches. "These are great."

"Becky—put those back," Regan commanded.

A crowd including Cynthia and Susan formed around Regan. "What about the show tomorrow?" someone asked.

"It's just a sprain, and my mom's being real cautious. She won't let me do the show this week, but I'll be okay for the next one."

People nodded their heads, talked about that day's history test, and wandered to their seats—all except Cynthia and Susan. They huddled in the back corner of the room, talking and occasionally looking up at Regan.

Mel cleared her throat. "They won't notice, huh?"

"Okay, they noticed, but they didn't give it any thought."

Mel looked at her doubtfully.

"All right. I won't take the splint off when I talk to Mrs. Vigil. I wasn't really going to, anyway. But I can still tell her the same things. It's most of the truth."

"Is it?" Mel questioned. "What about those blood tests?"

Regan flexed her left foot. The splint felt more and more uncomfortable. "I'm not going to worry about that weird doctor and his tests."

After third period, Regan found Mrs. Vigil in her room and got the reaction she was afraid of.

"Oh, no, Regan!" Mrs. Vigil cried. "Your knee again. Okay, what's all this?" she said, pointing to the splint. "Tell me what's going on."

"It's not as bad as it looks. It'll be okay." Regan sat down in front of Mrs. Vigil's desk as gracefully as she could.

Mrs. Vigil got up and moved next to her. "You've been telling me that for several weeks, but now this splint. What happened?"

"The doctor thinks I've sprained my knee." Regan glanced away. "He doesn't want me to walk on it for a few days, just to be on the safe side."

"I agree," Mrs. Vigil said. "Hmm. The show tomorrow. We'll have to cancel."

"I'm so sorry," Regan said. "I don't want to let you down. But I'll be fine by next week." She held her breath.

"Don't push it." Mrs. Vigil patted her shoulder. "I'm just glad you're going to a doctor now. We need to get that knee healed once and for all."

Mrs. Vigil moved to the blackboard and erased an English assignment. "You know what we need to do? You should have backup dancers. All dancers have understudies."

"Understudies?" Regan tried to keep her voice even.

"Not exactly understudies. Backup dancers. You know, two dancers behind you doing the routines every week. You choreograph the show, teach them, and then if you're sick, one of them can lead the show."

Regan breathed slowly. It had happened. Just what she'd feared. But she couldn't let Mrs. Vigil see how she felt. She *wouldn't* let Mrs. Vigil see how she felt. She smiled weakly. "What a great idea, Mrs. Vigil."

"Good. We'll announce it tomorrow. We can hold auditions Monday after school." Mrs. Vigil sat back at her desk. "You can help me choose the new dancers. You can do that Monday, even if your knee isn't ready."

Mrs. Vigil looked at Regan. "You're so creative, Regan. And you're marvelous on the show. But *Home-room Exercise* is not worth risking your long-term dance health."

"Thank you, Mrs. Vigil."

"You rest out tomorrow, and we'll see what your doctor says. Then next week you'll have your new partners to help you out. I think you'll really like working with other dancers."

"Yeah—great." Now, not only did she have to share the spotlight with someone else, she might lose out completely if Mrs. Vigil liked the others better. This week was going downhill fast.

During homeroom the following morning, the vice-principal announced the new audition, adding that Regan, along with Mrs. Vigil, would choose the backup dancers. A little cheer swelled around Cynthia's and Susan's desks.

The bell rang, and Regan clumped toward the door.

"Regan, wait up. How's your knee doing?"

Regan turned to see Cynthia calling. "Hey, Regan, how about sitting with us at lunch today?"

Chapter Nine

Mel sat with her arms folded over her chest and glared at Regan. "Try again. Go ahead and just try to tell me what we're doing spending Saturday afternoon in a movie theater, waiting for Cynthia and Susan to bring us popcorn."

"They invited us?" Regan said sheepishly.

"Cynthia invited you, and you know what she wants. I can't believe you're falling for it! Have you gone mad? Did the swelling move from your knee to your brain?" Mel turned to face Regan. "Cynthia invites you to lunch yesterday, treats you like you're one of her group, now this. I can't believe I let you talk me into coming."

"First of all, I didn't eat with them, and now, I'm just curious. They've ignored us for years—anyway, Cynthia has.

"Remember the pony party we weren't invited to? We said we didn't care, but I have to admit I was a little hurt. So now I just want to see what she's really like. She must have a nice side or no one would like her. And I want to know how far she'll go to convince me to choose them as the backup dancers. Play along with me on this one."

"You can't—" The lights dimmed, interrupting Mel's reply.

Cynthia and Susan tippy-toed sideways across Mel's feet to sit next to Regan and her crutches. They carried three Cokes, three large popcorns, and three boxes of Junior Mints.

They passed out the refreshments, excluding Mel. "Thanks, Cynthia," Regan said, "but where's Mel's?"

"Mel's? Ah—Susan just couldn't carry everything. She's going back. Susan?"

"But you said—"

Cynthia cut Susan off with a look.

"Be right back." Susan worked her way back down the aisle.

Watching Susan, Mel started to get up from her seat. "I can't do this."

Regan grabbed her hand and held her down. "I'll owe you big?" Her eyes pleaded with Mel.

"You'd better believe it."

Cynthia turned to Regan. "I've heard this movie is

cool," she said. She leaned closer to Regan. "So, like, what's the story with your knee?"

"It's going to be fine. The swelling was gone totally last night, or my mother wouldn't have let me come today. But I still have to wear this splint until Tuesday."

Mel whispered through clenched teeth, "If I were your mother, I wouldn't have let you come because you've lost your mind."

"Shsssh," the woman behind them said.

Cynthia giggled. "We'd better talk after." She turned her attention to the movie, and Susan returned with a jumbo popcorn and a Coke for Mel.

Afterward, they sat at McDonald's, drinking shakes. "Okay, okay, guys," Cynthia said. "Now tell us, do you know what we're going to have to do Monday for the audition? The announcement said you get to help choose the dancers, Regan."

"So—you two are going to audition again?"

"Sure we are," Cynthia answered. "The guys think it's cool, and I almost won the first time." She handed Regan more fries. "What do you think our chances are—Susan's and mine?"

"I'm sure Mrs. Vigil will have the final say. So I don't know."

"You'll have some influence, Regan," Cynthia persisted. "Mrs. Vigil has always liked you."

Regan could hear Mel mumbling under her breath.

Susan spoke. "Maybe you could ask her to put some stag leaps in it. Cynthia and I are good at stag leaps."

"Then you vote for us," Cynthia stated. "It's simple. Once we're on, we can hang out more. Go to parties, help with your clothes. You know—do stuff."

"Help her with her clothes?" Mel said. "Are you going to dress her every morning?"

"Regan doesn't need much help, Mel. But you could use the names of a few shops that don't sell only sporting goods." Cynthia got up from the table. "We'll see you at the audition Monday after school, Regan." They turned away and left.

"If that was an insult, she missed the mark. I like my clothes." Mel scrubbed the table with a napkin. "But can you believe *bribery*? Although I doubt she knows the word. I didn't think even Cynthia would stoop that low."

Regan sat stirring her melting shake with a straw. She'd never had anything before that someone else wanted so badly. "Yeah—pretty low," she said slowly.

"Are you going to tell Mrs. Vigil?"

"Mrs. Vigil? Oh, no. No point. The audition will be fair. They're on their own—I'm not going to do anything to help them—or to hurt them. Let's get out of here, Mel. Sorry I put you through this."

Monday arrived quickly. Regan hadn't even thought about her knee during the rest of the weekend. It was feeling so good, she hadn't even thought about the test results.

At the audition, eight dancers showed up to try out. Cynthia and Susan stood in the front row smiling at Regan.

"This will be fast today, dancers. Regan and I will make the decision, and the three of you can start working on Friday's show immediately," said Mrs. Vigil.

She turned to Regan. "Regan, I want you to walk through the routines using your crutches. Don't put *any* stress on your knee until you see the doctor tomorrow."

Regan nodded.

Mrs. Vigil gave the dancers time to learn the combo, then she and Regan began eliminating dancers. Soon they were down to Ann, Sylvia, Cynthia, and Susan. Cynthia and Susan were both on. But Cynthia's spark and flair made her stand out.

Mrs. Vigil spoke quietly to Regan. "Cynthia and Susan are looking good today—Cynthia in particular. She does have a certain quality."

Regan closed her eyes and took a deep breath. If it weren't for her dumb knee, she wouldn't have to choose. She wouldn't be sharing her show. Already, Mrs. Vigil was talking about Cynthia's striking presence. And Regan had to admit, Mrs. Vigil was right.

Cynthia had a Hollywood-style beauty, and it always created attention for her. But she possessed something else, something that drew people to her—when she wanted.

Regan didn't know what to do. She didn't want partners at all. But Mrs. Vigil seemed sold on the two of them. If they'd be consistent and dance like they just did, they'd be all right. They could keep up with her choreography if they didn't mess around.

Mrs. Vigil was waiting for her to come to a decision—and that day, Cynthia and Susan were the best of the group. "So you really think Cynthia and Susan could do the job?"

Mrs. Vigil nodded. "I do. The two of them could use this opportunity."

"All right, then." Regan swallowed. "Cynthia and Susan it is."

"It will be fine, Regan." Mrs. Vigil jotted a note on her clipboard, then turned to the students. "All right, dancers, once again, you were all wonderful. Thank you for auditioning. The backup dancers—to dance with Regan on the show and fill in if she is ill—will be . . . Cynthia Rider and Susan Walker."

"All right!" Cynthia and Susan slapped a high five.

"Congratulations, girls. The three of you get started on Friday's show. And Regan, be careful with your knee."

"Yes, ma'am. I will."

Mrs. Vigil picked up an armload of books and left the studio.

Cynthia loosened her thick ash-blond hair and shook her head. "Girls, this week's show will be a winner! Thanks, Regan. You made the right choice."

Regan looked at the ceiling. Mel was going to gag.

That first rehearsal with Cynthia and Susan felt a little awkward, but by the second afternoon they were working smoothly together, even with Regan on crutches. "See, you skip the left foot over to replace the right." Sitting on the tile floor of the wide hallway outside the gym, Regan demonstrated the movement with her hands. "At the same time circle both arms up around and down, then lunge on the right." She put weight on her right hand and bent her elbow as if it were her leg.

"Like this?" Cynthia performed the step.

"That's it," Regan said. "Then reverse it left, and do it again."

"That hand dancing works pretty well, Regan," Susan said.

"Maybe I should enter my hands in a talent show."

Cynthia lay on her stomach and ran her fingertips across the floor. "Do you think we could do our P.E. laps like this?"

"Dream on," Regan said.

"Are we done for the day, boss?" Cynthia rolled over to her pack.

Regan looked at her watch. "Yeah, we got pretty far."

Cynthia tossed bags of chips to the other two. "I saw Dustin and Ian right before rehearsal. They told me they can't wait to see us on the show." She handed out Cokes.

"The guys are going to go *crazy* over the hip section," Susan said.

"It's so easy to get them bothered." Cynthia giggled. "Okay, Regan. Who do you think is hot?"

Regan's cheeks grew warm. "No one in particular." She sipped her soda. "But after the first show, a lot of them sure started talking to me more."

"We need to choose someone for you to have a crush on," Cynthia said. "How about Corey? He's cute. And then there's Derrick. Or that new guy—he's got potential."

Regan laughed nervously.

"You've got to pick someone out. But not Dustin or Ian, they're ours."

"I'll remember that." Regan crumpled her empty chip bag. "Got to go. My mom's picking me up for a doctor's appointment. Hopefully I'll get rid of these crutches."

"Aw, no more hand dancing?" Cynthia teased.

"*That* I'll never give up. But these"—she shook her crutches as she got up—"I won't miss at all."

Thirty minutes later, she sat on the exam table, waiting for the doctor. Dr. Kruel entered and nodded to her mother. "Mrs. Shaffer." He flipped through some papers in a folder. Not looking at either of them, he began talking. "Your daughter doesn't need to wear the splint anymore. It doesn't appear to be an orthopedic problem."

Regan sighed with relief.

"But Mrs. Shaffer," Dr. Kruel continued, "the tests show some malformed lymphocytes in the fluid from the knee, and we need to rule out leukemia."

"Leukemia?" her mother said.

Regan's stomach twisted. She looked quickly from her mom to the doctor, and back to her mom again. Regan had heard the word before but wasn't quite sure what it was.

The doctor spoke with a cold and factual voice. "We will have to do a bone marrow test for a definitive diagnosis."

She couldn't have leukemia. She'd just hurt her knee. Her limp-o-whatevers were formed just fine.

The doctor looked at her mother. "Needless to say, all forms of cancer are serious. We must do the test immediately."

Regan couldn't speak. *Cancer?* Leukemia was *cancer?* No—this doctor was wrong.

"Mom, I want to go see Dr. Wills."

Her mother put her arms around Regan and gripped her tightly, saying, "The results must be wrong.

Can't you repeat the tests or do other blood work before we go all the way to a bone marrow test?"

"We've done all the preliminary tests, and they are accurate. The results indicate we must go to the next diagnostic step. The bone tap is the only way to confirm or rule out leukemia. The test itself takes only about five or ten minutes. A pathologist puts a needle into the back of the hipbone and draws out some of the marrow. It's painful, but it's quick."

Regan shouted, "A needle in my hip?" She bolted from her mother's arms. "I don't have cancer. Look, I just hurt my knee and it's not even swollen now. You don't know what you're talking about!"

Dr. Kruel looked at Regan for the first time. "The tests indicate otherwise." He shifted his gaze back to her mom. "It's imperative the bone marrow test is performed promptly."

Mrs. Shaffer spoke slowly. "Leukemia." Then she looked at Dr. Kruel with piercing eyes. "There's no other way to know for sure?"

"This is my recommendation."

Regan's mother sat down on the chair. "I—ah—I need to—we need to talk to my husband first—and Dr. Wills."

"As you wish. My nurse can answer any other questions and set up the appointment. Let her know what you decide."

Chapter Ten

An hour later at home, Regan leaned on her elbow at the kitchen table, her fist pressed against her mouth, listening to her mother talking to Dr. Wills. She could hear the strain in her mother's voice, a tone Regan had never heard before.

"You're saying you think this is the right course?" Mrs. Shaffer grabbed a short breath. "I see, it's just such a . . ." She nodded her head. "I understand. It's something that has to be ruled out." Her tone rose slightly. "It's just that Dr. Kruel was so blunt."

As her mother brought the conversation to a close, Regan's dad appeared at the door, home from work early. "We'll try not to worry. Thank you, Dr. Wills." She hung up the phone.

Regan looked up at her dad. A wave of sadness washed over her body.

She couldn't remember how they got home. They were just suddenly in the kitchen and her mom was talking on the phone.

Mr. Shaffer knelt next to Regan. "Okay, let's take this one step at a time. Your call was a little unclear," he said to Regan's mom.

"I know I didn't make much sense." Regan's mother shook her head back and forth. "I was in shock. The doctor just said the word *leukemia* with no warning." Her mother's voice got louder. "He doesn't know if it's cancer. He's irresponsible to tell us like that."

Regan's father stood and leaned his cheek against the top of Regan's head. He was warm and smelled of the spice soap he used. Then he sat down in the chair next to her.

"What exactly did they find?" he asked. "What makes them want to test for leukemia?"

Lowering her voice, her mother answered, "The fluid from her knee. Dr. Kruel said some lymphocytes found in the fluid from her knee are malformed." She continued, "And that it could indicate leukemia. He said leukemia was something to rule out." She started to get angry again. "He just barreled into the idea of cancer."

"What are this man's qualifications?" her father asked. "Dr. Wills recommended him, didn't she?"

"She did; yes, she did. And she says Dr. Kruel has a

terrible bedside manner." Mrs. Shaffer paused, then said, "But . . . she does say he knows his field."

"Does she agree with doing this test?"

Regan lifted her head and focused on her mother.

Mrs. Shaffer nodded. "Dr. Wills recommends we have the test. Do it and find out so we know what we're dealing with."

Mrs. Shaffer whispered under her breath, "Dear Lord, we'll do anything if you just make all this not true."

Regan pushed her chair back, holding the edge of the table as she stood. Quietly she said, "Make the arrangements for the test, Mom. I'm going to lie down for a while."

"Dinner. Regan, don't you want something to eat?" her mother asked. "I could fix you—"

"Thanks, Mom, but I'm not hungry."

Regan's dad wrapped his arms all the way around her, squeezing and rocking her back and forth. "I'm sorry, sweetheart, you're having to go through this. This could be a million other things. But if it is cancer, we will fight it. We'll handle it. The three of us together are stronger than any cancer cell. You remember that."

Regan felt her father's tears wet her forehead.

Regan had lain on her bed wearing her clothes and fallen asleep immediately. She woke up around midnight.

Her shoes were off and an extra blanket was draped over her. She couldn't remember anyone coming in to cover her up.

The whole afternoon was a fog but some of the numbness was wearing off. Did a doctor really tell her she might have cancer? Were her parents really worried it might be true?

She knew one fact—the bone marrow test. The nurse said the needle was really long. Well, she didn't use the words *really long,* but she said it was longer than a normal needle. It would have to be to get all the way into her hipbone and take out the insides of her bone.

She felt hot. She went to her chest of drawers and changed into pajamas. She wished she could make the test go away. Then she wished the test were scheduled for the next day instead of Thursday. The longer she waited, the bigger the needle would seem.

Her father was right. It could be a million things other than cancer. She shouldn't worry about something that wasn't a "for sure." But her father meant worrying about if she had leukemia or not. What worried Regan first was a "for sure." For sure, they were going to put a big sharp needle into her bone.

She'd lived through aches and pains from dancing, but a needle in her hip—ohhh. She got back in bed, said a prayer, closed her eyes, and hoped for sleep.

Chapter Eleven

Regan slowly entered homeroom the next morning and walked to her desk. A group of kids listening to Becky abruptly scattered when she passed, looking like startled rabbits.

"Settle down, people. Settle down." The homeroom teacher stood at the front of the room. "You need a dark pencil to fill out this survey. I have extras if you don't have a dark leaded pencil. This is a survey for . . ."

When Regan looked up, Becky was whispering to the girl in front of her. When she finally paused to take a breath, the other girl turned around to smile at Regan with a pitiful look.

Regan tried to concentrate on her questionnaire, but people kept looking at her when they thought she wouldn't notice.

When the bell rang, Regan picked up her books

and fled. But someone from Cynthia's group stopped her with a hug. "Regan, I'm so sorry to hear about the cancer. I'm sure the chemotherapy will work—not everybody dies from cancer, you know."

"What? Is that why everybody is acting so—"

"My mom's got a wig that's about the same color as your hair. You can borrow it when your hair falls out." As quickly as the assault ended, the girl left.

Cynthia and Susan appeared in her place. "Regan," Cynthia said, "you don't have to worry about a thing. We'll take over until you get better."

"That's not going to be necessary."

"And that Becky is a real piece of work," Cynthia continued. "Do you know she's telling everybody? Even people you don't know."

Regan exploded. "Becky's such an idiot. I don't have cancer. I'm not going to have chemotherapy, and I'm not dying." She wiped the sweat from her upper lip. "I'm just fine. Look at my leg. It couldn't be better. I'll be at rehearsal this afternoon, ready to dance. And please do me a favor. Stop Becky's stupid rumors!"

Regan struggled through the day, putting up with stares and whispers and setting people straight. Mel helped her run damage control, but she felt exhausted by the time she got to rehearsal that afternoon.

"Let's start with this set of stomach exercises. I know people hate stomach exercises, but these are kind of fun. I'll tell the kids to partner up, and then this is what we'll do. One partner lies down." Regan lay down on the hall floor. "The other person stands with his feet on each side of the first person's head, facing his feet. The person on the ground holds the standing person's ankles and lifts both of his own legs straight up in the air." Regan put her arms on the floor above her head and lifted her legs up. "The standing guy pushes the floor guy's legs hard toward the floor, and the floor guy stops his legs from touching the floor and quickly brings them back up for the standing guy to do it again. It's great for the lower stomach muscles.

"Susan, come here and I'll show you."

Susan took only one step before Cynthia stopped her. "Let's you and I do it together." Cynthia got down on the floor. "How does it go?"

Susan walked over to Cynthia.

Regan swallowed hard before she spoke again. "Sure—you guys do it together." She quietly talked them through it.

"How do you come up with your ideas, Regan?" Cynthia asked.

"I don't know," Regan answered without enthusiasm. "Some stuff I learn in class, other stuff I make up."

"Do you always set up the show in the same order? A warm-up first, right?"

Regan nodded.

Cynthia continued to probe the entire rehearsal.

By the time Regan got home, she'd had enough of questions and wanted to be alone. But her parents insisted upon dinner and kept trying to get her to talk. Regan had only one question. "Mom, did you tell me everything the doctor said?"

"Of course, sweetheart," her mother said.

Her father added, "We wouldn't keep anything from you, Regan. We're going through this together."

Regan believed her parents, but she was still more and more depressed. She crawled into bed and pulled the covers to her chin. She dreaded the needle torture test the next morning. And everyone, except Mel, had treated her so weirdly all day.

Cynthia's standoffishness at rehearsal wouldn't have been odd before, but the three of them had been having fun together. Regan liked being included in Cynthia and Susan's boy talk. She and Mel never talked about boys—Mel liked to talk about sports and homework.

But that afternoon, there hadn't been any boy talk—it was all strictly business. When rehearsal was over, they were out of there. And what was with Cynthia stopping Susan from doing the stomach exercise with her? Could Cynthia actually believe they could catch leukemia from her? Blast that Becky and her big mouth.

A quiet knock came from her bedroom door. Regan didn't answer, but the door slowly opened anyway. Mel peeked around the edge of the door. "Can I come in?"

"Hey, what's going on?" Regan felt the start of a smile.

Mel's lucky soccer ball key chain dangled beside the sleeping bag she carried. "I thought you might need help studying for your big test tomorrow."

Chapter Twelve

"Regan, we'll try to make this as comfortable for you as we can," Dr. Sanchez, the pathologist, said calmly. "I'll numb the area, but I can't numb bone."

Regan lay facedown on the exam table and swallowed roughly.

"It will take two or three shots to anesthetize the layers of tissue, so I need you to hang in there. The first will be the most difficult, then it should get easier."

There were only three things that would make that moment easier for Regan—not doing it, Dr. Sanchez not being so cute, or getting to keep her panties on for the test.

The nurse spoke. "Regan, I'm going to open the back of the gown so that we can begin."

"Your mom and I are right here, Twinkle Toes. It's

going to be all right." Her dad's comforting voice came from above her head.

She felt the tie loosen on the side of her gown and the nurse push the light cotton material off her rear.

When her dad said he'd be with her at the test, she didn't realize she'd be showing him her naked backside. Her face burned, but she wanted her dad with her.

"They tell me you're a dancer. What kind?" Dr. Sanchez rubbed something cold on her left hip, then covered the area with what felt like a light cloth.

Regan cleared her throat. "Ah—ballet . . . jazz . . ."

"Okay, Regan, now a sharp prick."

Regan gasped. She gripped her mother's hand and willed herself into steady breaths. The sharpness of the needle dulled. She forced the image of the needle digging into her hip out of her mind.

"Squeeze my hand as hard as you want," her mother said.

"Are you okay, Regan?" Dr. Sanchez asked.

"It's okay. I'm fine."

"Okay. We're going to go deeper now. Here we go."

Regan prepared herself for the sharp pain, but it didn't come when the needle entered.

"Do you like ballet or jazz best?"

"Both . . . both really, but probably ballet the . . . aghhh!" Fire seared through her hip, then receded.

"Can you feel anything now?" asked Dr. Sanchez.

Regan felt tugging where the needle was but nothing else. "No, not really."

"You're doing great. Now, Regan, this next part is going to be a little rougher. I need you to stay very still. As I explained earlier, you will feel pressure on your body and the pain will be intense, but it won't last long."

Regan's mother held her hand tightly. "Hold on, sweetheart. It will be over soon."

Regan nodded her head.

"Okay, here we go," Dr. Sanchez said.

The nurse spoke. "Regan, breathe deeply and evenly."

Regan couldn't feel the big needle going into her skin, but she knew it was there. She was glad they didn't show her the needle, and she sure didn't look.

Regan could feel Dr. Sanchez leaning way over her body on the table. Then she felt it. He used his weight to push the big needle into her bone. Burning pain ripped through her body.

A ratcheting sound filled her ears and tiny vibrations waved through her hipbone. Then she felt the needle sucking the insides of her bone out. When was he going to stop? She felt as if her hipbone might collapse.

When the pain stopped, Regan heard a whimpering sound.

"Stay on your stomach just a little while longer, Regan," the nurse said. "We've got to keep pressure on it until you stop bleeding."

Dr. Sanchez added, "All the aspirin you've been taking for your inflammation has thinned your blood. You did great, Regan. Just lie there and try to relax while the bleeding stops."

Her mom blotted with a Kleenex under Regan's eyes and then handed her the tissue.

"You did it, Regan. It's over," her father crooned while stroking her hair. "You did it. It's all over, Twinkle Toes."

Regan did not realize she was crying. The whimpering she had heard must have been hers.

Dr. Sanchez spoke. "Your doctor will call you in the morning with the results and will answer any questions."

"The morning!" Regan stopped crying. "I can't wait another day! They didn't say I'd have to wait."

"I'm sorry, Regan. I know this is difficult." Dr. Sanchez tried to comfort her. "I'll leave an urgent note on the call instructions. Your doctor will let you know immediately when he gets the results."

Regan started crying again. She'd already waited two days—she just couldn't wait another. Her breathing got quick and shallow and she began gasping for air. Where was the air? There was no air. It had all left the room.

"Regan. Breathe slowly. Regan! Nurse!" Regan's mother yelled.

A nurse appeared beside Regan. "Regan, be calm. Breathe in through your nose and out through your mouth. Breathe in." The nurse inhaled with her. "Breathe out." The nurse exhaled with her. "Breathe in—breathe out. That's it. That's better. The bleeding has stopped so you can sit up now—slowly." Somehow they got her sitting up with her legs dangling off the exam table.

And somehow her parents got her out of the hospital and home—to wait. Regan used to think waiting for audition results was difficult, but waiting to find out if she had cancer was just cruel.

After a sleepless night, the three of them sat at the kitchen table by the phone.

Regan said nothing. Finally she broke the silence. "Mom, am I going to die?"

Her mother's eyes filled with tears. "You are *not* going to die!" She squeezed Regan's hand. "You don't have cancer. And when this is over, I'm going to report that doctor."

Regan's father kissed her forehead. "We're going to find out what's wrong and take care of you. You are *not* going to die."

Regan looked from her father to her mother. Her dad's face was calm, while her mom's held back tears. She felt confused and afraid.

Would dying hurt? Would it hurt more than the big needle in her hip? Or would it be something beautiful—her spirit dancing for eternity?

The phone rang, and all three of them jumped. Regan's dad answered the phone. He nodded his head twice. "There's no question?" he asked. "Thank you—thank you, doctor."

Mr. Shaffer hung up the phone. A weary smile crossed his lips. "Negative. The test is negative."

"Do I have cancer?"

"No." Her father shook his head. "You don't have leukemia. You don't have cancer."

Regan looked at her parents and cried.

That night, neighbors and people from the Shaffers' church dropped by to say they were glad everything was all right. Many of them brought food and stayed to visit, including Becky and her mother.

Becky had been in the kitchen with the food, but now she hurtled into the living room with her hands and mouth full of potato chips and headed straight for the couch. "Isn't this great! I love parties." She turned and plopped down next to Regan.

"*Ow.*" Regan winced.

"Hey, Becky, be careful. She still hurts from yesterday. Move over a little." Mel motioned Becky over.

"Sorry, I didn't mean to hurt you. I just thought everything was all right now."

"Everything *is* all right, and I'd appreciate you not telling the whole school I'm dying the next time I have a cold or something."

Mel spoke before Becky could. "But did they say why your knee did an imitation of a blowfish?"

"They don't have any idea—especially since my knee's fine now. Mom wanted to report Dr. Kruel, but Dr. Wills talked her out of it. She said he followed proper procedure, and that you can't report someone for being insensitive."

"That rule needs to be changed," Mel declared. "He's a jerk. And can you believe with a name like Kruel anyone actually hires him for their doctor?"

"That should have been our first clue," Regan said. "But all I really care about now is my knee. Dr. Wills said we'd just wait and watch. Maybe it will never happen again."

Becky jumped back into the conversation. "But isn't it great how everyone's brought you all this food and stuff?" She shoved more potato chips into her mouth and continued talking. "My mom made a chocolate cake when she heard you didn't have cancer. She wouldn't let me have any until she brought it to you first."

"The only other time I've ever seen something like this," Mel said, "was when my aunt's mother—no, I mean my aunt's husband's mother—died. Their house was full of people for days."

"See what I mean? Becky had everyone believing I was dying! This proves it."

"Look on the bright side," Becky said. "You're not dead, and you still get a party."

Mel broke in. "Beck. Why don't you go get some more food for that mouth of yours?"

"Good idea. You guys want anything? I'll bring you some stuff." Becky popped up from the couch and headed for the kitchen.

Mel giggled. "That girl doesn't have a clue. Talk about needing to report someone to an insensitivity board."

"She drives me crazy." Regan's eyes watered. "She is right about one thing, though. I'm not dying."

"Thank goodness." Mel sighed. "I didn't want to have to scrape up a new best friend. It would be hard to find someone who could cheer as loud as you do at the Dr. King Day soccer tournament."

"That's all I mean to you—a pair of screaming lungs?"

Mel looked squarely into Regan's eyes. "Well, maybe you mean a bit more, but I can't tell you because it'll go to your head."

She smiled at Mel and then shifted her weight to the edge of the seat cushion. "My lungs and I will be the noisiest ones there. Come on, let's make a banner to cover the wall above the couch. Let's call this party the I Don't Have Leukemia Party!"

"You sit. I'll get the paper and markers." Mel dashed away.

Two ladies from church filled the vacant spots on the couch. "We're so relieved, dear, that you're going to be all right. Your mother, bless her soul, has been worried sick and . . ."

At that moment, Regan's mother and father came out of the kitchen. She excused herself and got up carefully from the couch. She walked across the room and tightly wrapped her arms around them both.

Chapter Thirteen

"It's great getting everything back to normal again. Your being sick was creepy." Mel held up a sports magazine to Regan and pointed to an ad. "Do you think these Nikes would help me on the court?"

"You don't need any help with basketball, but your wardrobe could use a shot in the arm." Regan shivered. "Do you want a sweatshirt? It's cold."

"No," Mel replied. "I'm fine."

Regan pulled on her dancing legs sweatshirt. She felt clammy as she wrapped her arms around her body for warmth. "Your wardrobe is one of the reasons I wanted you to come over tonight. I've invited—"

Regan was cut off when her bedroom door opened and Cynthia and Susan marched into the room with their arms full of shopping bags.

"Okay, okay. I know we're late, but some of this stuff was hard to find." Cynthia dropped her sacks on the bed next to Regan.

Cynthia looked great. Her jeans were ripped at both knees. She wore a black turtleneck with a southwestern vest done in an Indian blanket pattern of reds, blues, oranges, and yellows. And best of all, she wore black motorcycle boots with pointy toes and wide leather straps around the ankles held together with a silver ring.

"Look at the outrageous stuff Cynthia found." Susan pulled the rewards of their Saturday shopping from the bags.

"I know what these are"—Regan held up a pair of baggy plaid shorts—"but what are these?" Regan examined a piece of white lace with two clips attached to the bottom and one clip on the top.

Cynthia giggled. "Garters, my dear."

Mel sat wide-eyed with eyebrows raised. "What are *they* doing here?" she demanded.

"That's what I started to tell you. I invited Cynthia and Susan to come over tonight, too. Cynthia had a great idea for an outfit that will be really different."

Cynthia opened a package of white panty hose, but there was no panty attached to the legs. "Stockings!" Cynthia announced.

Regan started laughing. "I give. How do we put this together?"

"Simple." Cynthia instructed, "We'll wear the stockings and the shorts and attach them together with the garters. Cool or what?"

"Hot!" Susan agreed while tugging off her motorcycle boots that matched Cynthia's.

Mel coughed loudly. "Cold is more like it, but that's beside the point. Regan, weren't you and I spending the evening together?"

"We're just here as fashion consultants," Cynthia said.

"For who?"

Cynthia tossed Mel a package of stockings. "Regan said to bring enough for four."

"She did, did she?"

"I just thought it would be fun for us to—"

"You know what? You guys have a good time. See you later, Regan." Mel took off down the hallway.

Regan looked at Cynthia. "Don't leave. I'll be right back."

She caught up with Mel in the foyer before she'd reached the front door. "Mel, don't go. If you'd just try, the four of us could have a lot of fun together."

"Sewing garter belts onto shorts in December is not my idea of a fun evening." Mel leaned back against the door. "Why didn't you tell me they were coming?"

"Because you wouldn't have come otherwise."

"You got that one right." Mel ran her hand across her hair. "How did they get to you?"

"They didn't *get* to me, Mel, it's just that they really are fun. Doing the show with them yesterday turned out better than I thought it would. The energy was incredible. But, Mel, you're my best friend. I just want all of us to be friends together."

"Well, dream on. There's no way I'm going to be friends with those fluff balls. A few months ago you wouldn't have been caught dead being friends with them, either!"

"Please, just give them a chance. We're older now. I like being with them. And I want you included, too." Regan took a breath. "Mel, soon you'll be interested in the things we talk about—like boys and clothes. I just want you to be ready."

"Ready? Ready for what?"

Mel's eyes shifted and looked behind Regan. Regan turned.

"What's going on here? Your father and I could hear you two all the way back in our study." Mrs. Shaffer walked toward the girls. "What's the problem?"

"Nothing, Mom. Just a . . . just a difference of opinion."

"Mel?" Mrs. Shaffer tilted her head questioningly.

Mel glanced at Regan. "Yeah, just a difference of opinion."

"Mel looks pretty upset for a difference of opinion."

"It's okay, Mom."

"I hope you get it settled before Christmas Eve," Mrs. Shaffer said. "Because your mother and I have already started planning a walking tour around Old Town to see the luminarias after supper."

Mel finally smiled a little. "That does sound fun."

"Good. We'll plan on it." Regan's mother looked at them a moment. "Do you need any help?"

"Thanks, Mom, but we'll be all right."

"Okay, Regan. Good night, Mel." Mrs. Shaffer went back to the study.

Regan turned back to Mel. "Please stay?"

Mel shook her head. "No. Your mom being nice doesn't change things. Don't invite them next time, okay?" She opened the door and left.

Chapter Fourteen

On the first day of class after the holidays, Regan and Mel met early at the DVTV studio. Regan sat on the cold tile floor, slowly opening and closing her fingers into fists. Stiff. It must be the January cold.

The holidays had gone pretty well, except Mel and she hadn't seen each other as much as they usually did. They did see each other on Christmas Eve, which was like old times. They had walked, side by side, in beautiful Old Town, bundled up in down coats against the icy air. The old adobe church and shops surrounding the square of the original Albuquerque had been lined with glowing luminarias. The candles in the small paper sacks had flickered and lit the way for the Christ child.

Regan had hoped that evening would change Mel's mind about spending time with her and Cynthia and

Susan. It hadn't. So Regan hadn't seen Mel again until the first day of school. Mel had only agreed to meet her in the TV studio because Cynthia and Susan wouldn't be around that early.

Regan lay back onto the studio floor. She pulled her right knee to her chest, stretched the other leg straight, and looked over at Mel. "Missed you last week."

Mel didn't answer right away.

Regan turned her eyes from her and the chilly silence that had nothing to do with the January weather.

Finally Mel broke the quiet. "Yeah, well, at least we had Christmas Eve together."

Regan unfolded her right leg toward the ceiling and pulled until her shin touched her nose. "It was beautiful, wasn't it?" She flexed and rotated her foot. "Maybe . . . we could fit in a movie this weekend?"

"With your exercise buddies? No thanks."

"No, just the two of us."

Mel looked skeptical.

"Really, just us."

"Well, if you think you can spare the time . . ." Mel stopped herself, then looked pleased. "Sounds good to me."

"What sounds good?" Susan's voice darted into the quiet room.

"Reporting for rehearsal, sir." Cynthia dropped her dance bag and books on the floor.

Mel got to her feet. "See you in homeroom."

"Hey, Mel. Hang around awhile," Regan said.

"No. I've got stuff to do. Later."

Cynthia walked over to Regan. "Guess what I just heard?"

"What's that?" Regan flopped over to her stomach and pushed her back into an arch.

"Dancewear Unlimited, that to-die-for leotard shop, has heard about our show and wants to sponsor us. They give us a new outfit every month, and get this—we keep everything!" Cynthia and Susan started a squeal of glee that accelerated with their unison bouncing.

Regan jumped up off the floor. "This is incredible."

Cynthia spoke breathlessly. "We're to go over on Martin Luther King Jr. Day to pick out tights, leotards, shoes, the whole package! Then let's do lunch and a movie. Totally cool!"

Wow, Regan thought. People outside the school knew about the show. She rubbed her stiff hands. This was getting better than she'd ever dreamed.

Two weeks later Regan watched through her bedroom window for Susan's car. Susan's mother had offered to drive them over to pick out their new workout clothes. She was ready early and sat writing in her journal. The quote at the top of the page read:

We look at the dance to impart the sensation of living in an affirmation of life, to energize the spectator into keener awareness of the vigor, the mystery, the humor, the variety, and the wonder of life.

—Martha Graham

She continued writing:

> The last two weeks have been wonderful. It's like when a really bad headache finally goes away and you realize how good you feel without pain.
>
> I had been holding myself so stiff and tight, not eating or sleeping well. I was like Eeyore, from Winnie the Pooh, with bad news following me everywhere.
>
> But now that I'm on the other side of the cancer scare I know how lucky my life really is. No problems, no great tragedies.

Regan looked out of her bedroom window just as a car pulled up to the curb. She closed the journal, grabbed her coat, and headed for the front door. But by the time she'd walked out into the cold, bright January morning, a Jeep had pulled into the driveway.

Mel! Ohhh, no—the soccer tournament! How could she have forgotten to tell Mel she couldn't go? Mel would kill her.

"Come on, Regan," Mel called from the Jeep. She

turned to look at the other car. "Is that Cynthia and Susan over there? They're not going with us?"

"No, they're not going with us—Mel, I'm so sorry. I forgot to tell you. We've got to go to Dancewear Unlimited this morning to get our outfits for the show. The shop is sponsoring us. Isn't that cool?"

"You forgot to tell me, or you forgot the tournament, or both? Whatever it was, you'll have to get your stuff later."

"I—I—Mel, I'm going to have to miss the morning game and try to make it in the afternoon. I really need to go with Cynthia and Susan. I don't want them choosing the leotards without me. I'm sorry—I'll make it up to you."

"Fine. Go with your friends."

"Mel, I'll get there as soon as I can, okay?" Regan got into the backseat of Susan's car. Her stomach twisted into a sour knot.

Chapter Fifteen

A few days later, Regan overheard her mother talking on the phone. "Hi, Mel, is your mother home? Would you ask her to please give me a call when she gets in?"

Mrs. Shaffer was silent a moment. "Thank you, Mel. Oh, by the way, we've missed you around here. Why don't you come to dinner tonight?" Silence again. "Oh—I see." Her mother listened to the phone, then spoke again. "I'm so sorry, sweetheart. I know. . . . Don't you think you could—" Regan's mother's voice stopped short. "I understand."

Mrs. Shaffer continued, "I hope the two of you work it out soon." Another pause. "I understand. I won't say anything. Bye, Mel."

Regan quietly inched her way back down the hall to her bedroom. How were they going to work it out if Mel wouldn't speak to her? She had gone over to the soccer field to catch the second game, but Mel wasn't there, since her team had lost that morning. Then Regan had tried her house—Mel wouldn't come to the door. She had called Mel three times that night, and she wouldn't talk. Then, Tuesday at school, Mel had ignored her.

At least Mel had brought up the subject to Regan's mom on the phone. Maybe that was a good sign. Maybe Mel just needed a little space and time to cool off. But she'd already had two weeks—and they still hadn't talked.

Regan stood in the deserted hallway after school and read a note taped to Mrs. Vigil's closed door.

> *Regan,*
>   *I had to go to the office. I'll be back in about 10 min. Please wait in my room.*
>
>   *Thanks,*
>   *Mrs. Vigil*

Regan entered the empty classroom and shut the door. Her eyes surveyed the room before she sauntered toward the chalkboard decorated with a string of Valentine hearts. Not all the teachers decorated for the holidays, but Mrs. Vigil always put something up.

She moved around the teacher's desk and slid into the center seat in the front row. She wished Mrs. Vigil were one of her teachers at Desert Vista. Mel had her for Lang/Lit and thought she was great.

The door to the classroom opened. "Good. You're here, Regan. Sorry I had to step out a moment." Mrs. Vigil put a stack of papers on her desk and then sat next to Regan with a mug of tea in her hands.

"Young lady, I'm so impressed with what you've done with *Homeroom Exercise*. You are a marvelous choreographer."

Regan felt a smile spread across her face. "I *love* making up dances of my own. It's different from learning your dances, Mrs. Vigil. I don't mean I don't like your dances, it's just that . . ."

"I know what you mean, Regan." Mrs. Vigil chuckled. "It feels different when you perform your own vision of how movement should fit to the music."

"That's it exactly. It feels like more of me. The dance comes from my brain as well as my body when I do the choreography." Regan sighed. "And that feels good."

"I'm glad you like what you're doing," Mrs. Vigil said, "because all the students like it as well. They like it so much that teachers from other schools have heard about the show and have made inquiries at the main office. And guess what? The music coordinator has decided to broadcast the show to all the middle schools in the city."

"You're kidding!" Regan leaned toward Mrs. Vigil. "*All* the middle schools? Everybody will be watching the show? I don't believe it!"

"Well, believe it. They're going to start the first week in March. Then, instead of going through the closed-circuit system here at the school, you'll go down to Channel 3 and do your show from there."

"This is so cool!" Regan's feet danced around under the desk.

Mrs. Vigil smiled. "You know, I shouldn't be surprised the show is such a hit. Regan, you have an enormous gift. Your natural talent as a dancer was obvious to me at your first ballet class when you were eight years old."

Regan's cheeks warmed.

"But natural talent is easy," Mrs. Vigil said. "It's something you're born with. It's not something you have to work for."

Regan's warm feeling faded. She had no idea where Mrs. Vigil was heading.

Mrs. Vigil leaned back in the desk chair and continued. "What I'm really impressed by is something more difficult to achieve, something very unusual for a twelve-year-old: Your ability to focus—to apply yourself every day to things that are important to you. Things like your dance and schoolwork, of course, but also your kindness and fairness to people. These are things you have to make daily choices about. I know that's not always easy."

Did Mrs. Vigil know she and Mel were having problems? Regan didn't know what to say.

"For instance"—Mrs. Vigil crossed her arms over her chest—"Cynthia."

Oh, no, Regan thought.

"Cynthia doesn't always make the best choices. I've known her as long as I've known you, Regan. She's talented, and I want her to develop that talent and learn something about personal relationships. That's one reason I thought it would be good for the two of you to work together. But don't let Cynthia swallow you up."

"She won't, Mrs. Vigil. We're getting along pretty well, and I keep trying to get Mel involved with us, but she won't—"

"Don't give up on Mel. She's too much like you for you to lose her friendship. She's another person with focus."

Regan sighed—she'd gone from elation to desolation in five minutes.

"Well." Mrs. Vigil stood up. "I know you'll work all this out. In the meantime, congratulations on the show. You've got three weeks to get it ready for the big time. I know the three of you will be great."

"Thanks, Mrs. Vigil," Regan said quietly. "Thanks for everything."

That night Regan turned over in her bed. "Ohhh . . ." A straitjacket kept her from moving her arms and legs, and firecrackers exploded in her joints. What a weird dream.

"Owww . . ." Regan forced herself to roll to her back and open her eyes to a slit. A stiff, achy feeling pressed her body down. She was burning hot and dripping with sweat. She must have the flu. She tried to curl up on her side, but a noise that sounded like a whimpering new puppy escaped from her.

What was wrong with her? She tried to get into a sitting position, but intense pain caused her arms to give way, and she fell back on the bed.

"Mom," Regan called. A shot of needles prickled through her shoulders. This time she yelled, *"Mom— oww."*

"Regan—Regan, what's wrong?" Her mother flew into her bedroom.

"Mom—I'm sick."

"What's the matter?"

"I don't know. I hurt everywhere."

Her father entered the room and stood behind her mother. "What hurts, Regan?"

"My legs, my hips, my shoulders—everything."

Regan's mother said, "She's burning up, Steven. I'm calling the doctor."

"I'll get a cold cloth and Tylenol." Her father was already on his way.

In the middle of the pain traveling through her body like electricity speeding through wire, Regan's bladder burned. She willed her feet to touch the floor and fought through the pain to stand. Her hips spasmed. She shrieked and collapsed to the floor.

Her mother ran into the room. "Steven, Steven!" she yelled. "Call 911." She rushed to her side. "Oh my God, what in the world is wrong? What's happening?"

Regan closed her eyes against the pain. Her pajama bottoms, warm and wet, stuck to her thighs.

Chapter Sixteen

Why won't they answer me? Regan wanted her eyes open.

"Nurse, how much longer do you think she'll be out?"

Regan felt her mother's lips on her forehead. She tried to reach out.

"A few more hours and she should start coming around."

Dry—her tongue was stuck. Drifting . . . drifting . . . drifting down the stream . . .

Someone held her hand. Regan twitched a finger.

"Regan? Regan, sweetheart, it's Mom."

She separated her lips. "Water."

"Just a sip." Her father held a cup to her lips.

Hospital. Merrily, merrily, merrily, merrily, pain is not a dream. She opened her eyes. "More water, please."

"There you are." Her dad stroked her bangs over. "Are you back with us?"

"Yeah . . ." Regan moved her hand across the warm bed—a waterbed. At least she could move her arm without feeling broken glass tumbling inside her shoulder. She looked at her father. "It is cancer, isn't it?"

"No, Regan. It's definitely not cancer." Before he could continue, the hospital room door opened.

"Hi there, young lady."

"Dr. W.," Regan said quietly. "You were here with me last night, weren't you?"

"That I was, and I'm really glad to see you awake." She moved over and patted Regan's hand. Her dress was the color of Dad's red geraniums and a pink stethoscope was draped around her neck. "Are you resting more comfortably this morning?"

Mrs. Shaffer answered, "She seems better."

"Have you talked to the rheumatologist yet?" Regan's father asked.

"Yes. Dr. Rich wants to do more tests. He says nothing definitive has shown up yet."

"Regan," her father said evenly, "the doctors think you may have arthritis."

"*Arthritis?*" Her head cleared. "How can I have arthritis? Old people get arthritis."

"Not this kind," Dr. Wills said. "This is JRA, juvenile rheumatoid arthritis. It's a type kids get."

Regan stared at her. She couldn't say a thing.

"Regan, Dr. Rich thinks you had what he calls an acute flare. That's a sudden onset of arthritis with several joints getting inflamed at the same time and causing the kind of pain you were having. Your tests a couple of months ago didn't indicate JRA, but it's looking more like a good possibility."

"He doesn't know for sure?"

"Arthritis is difficult to diagnose," Dr. Wills said. "Many times the first tests falsely indicate leukemia or other illnesses—like what happened to you. Dr. Rich wants to do more tests to be absolutely sure. Regan, you're going to have to stay in the hospital a few days."

"I can't do that! I can't miss the show again!" Regan said sharply.

"I'm sorry, you'll have to this week." Dr. Wills continued, "We've got to try to find out what's going on, and you've got to be able to walk before you can dance."

Regan dug her fingernails into the warm plastic of the waterbed.

Dr. Wills reached over and stroked Regan's right hand until she relaxed it. "You're going to be all right, Regan." She spoke to Regan's parents as she headed for the door. "Dr. Rich will be in soon to explain how we should proceed. I'll check in with you later."

Regan clawed the mattress again. Maybe she could puncture the waterbed with her nails. It would make a real mess.

The next day, Regan slowly awakened from a nap. She lay in a regular hospital bed with her eyes closed, listening to sounds. Carts wheeled up and down the carpeted hallway, sterile metal scissors clanked against sterile metal bowls, and two hushed voices in her room spoke in serious tones. Regan listened as her parents talked.

"I don't know what this will do to her, Lana," Regan's father said. "A dancer is all she's ever wanted to be. If arthritis makes that difficult, I just don't know. . . ."

"Steven, we don't know how bad it might get. She may have a mild form, or she may not have it at all. What I'm focusing on is that she doesn't have cancer. She can live with arthritis."

"Yes, she can live, but will she really be alive without her dance?"

"You're looking too far ahead, Steven. Let's take this one step at a time. We don't know anything for sure yet.

"Come on," her mother added. "Let's go get some tea. She probably won't be awake for a while."

Regan listened to her mother and father leave the room. She opened her eyes and sat up in bed.

Regan hadn't thought about this being permanent.

She carefully reached for the table and rolled it closer. Stiffly, she wrote on a pad of paper:

3. **Foul Up Dancing Career**
   a. burn with fire in every joint of my body
   b. learn to walk with a walker
   c. spend days in the hospital
   d. develop a health problem the doctors can't figure out

Regan pulled the paper from the pad and used it to blot a small teardrop from the corner of her eye. Then she worked a rip down the middle of the paper. She shredded the paper faster and faster until it got so small her nails scratched the pads of her fingers. She stared at the pile of confetti she had created.

"Nice job," a voice said softly from the door. "What deserves such a thrashing?"

Regan looked up. It was Mel.

"Can I come in?" Mel asked.

"Sure." Regan smiled for the first time in two days, but the smile slipped off her face as fast as it came. "If—you want to, that is."

Mel entered and sat in a chair next to the bed. "Your mom called me yesterday after school. Well, actually,

Becky had told me before that something was wrong, and you were in the hospital."

"Miss Know-It-All *would* have the news first."

"Yeah, well, I would have come by last night, but your mom said today would be better."

Regan adjusted herself in the bed. "You're here. That's all that matters."

"I just wanted to see if you were all right. That's all. I'm going to take off now."

"Look, Mel," Regan said plainly. "I'm sorry. I was a real jerk."

Mel crossed her arms over her chest. "Ah, the girl has some intelligence left after all."

"Can we start over? Please?"

"We'll see." Mel's lips formed a tight little grin. "But you'll have to start with probation."

"Anything you say, Judge."

Mel sat on Regan's bed. "Okay, so what happened?"

"My entire body was taken over by an alien. I couldn't walk. My hands were so swollen I couldn't make a fist."

"You must have been terrified," Mel said.

"I was." Regan cleared her throat. "But now I'm just mad. This is keeping me from the show and dancing, and I just want it to be over."

"What is this? What's wrong with you?" Mel demanded.

"They think I have arthritis."

"Arthritis!" Mel looked at Regan with disbelief. "You're too young for arthritis."

"It's a kind kids get," Regan answered. "They don't know for sure, but they're still giving me medicine for it and some exercises to keep my joints from getting too stiff."

"Well, you're better now," Mel said. "So the treatments must be working."

"That's what I think, too."

Regan looked at the plant beside her bed. Her father had brought the fuchsia to her that morning. Its flowers cascaded gracefully over the basket.

"My dad's really scared about this."

"Of course he is. Parents are supposed to worry. It's in their job description."

Regan smiled—Mel was back.

Chapter Seventeen

Regan looked out of her hospital room window at the Sandias. That morning a breeze moved late-winter clouds across the mountain like ghosts in a parade. She longed to be out of the hospital and in her home at the foot of the mountains.

It was her third day in the hospital. If Dr. Rich agreed, she might go home that night.

Regan wondered what would happen about this week's *Homeroom Exercise*. Would Mrs. Vigil cancel the show, or have Cynthia and Susan do it? She wasn't sure they could pull it off on their own.

But for now, all Regan cared about was getting out of the hospital and back to the show as soon as possible. Dr. Rich said managing her pain and taking control of her recovery was her responsibility. So she had work to do.

Opening the pamphlet from the physical therapist, Regan carefully worked through each exercise. At first, she couldn't see how they could help; they were all so simple. But since she'd started them the day before, she'd felt more control with a lot less pain. However, she didn't know if it was the pain medication or the exercises that helped more.

Regan placed her forearm firmly on top of the table, with her hand hanging over the edge. She bent her wrist up as far as it would go and held it. Then she bent her wrist down as far as possible.

The exercise was simple, but not easy. The day before, she made a poor excuse for a wave. This one would pass for a decent greeting.

Next—her fingers. She laid her hand flat on the table and slowly curled her fingers in to form a fist, then just as slowly returned the hand to a flat, open position. Doing this reminded Regan of a time-lapse film she had seen of a rose opening.

A quiet knock made her look up. Cynthia and Susan stood in the doorway. She quickly closed the pamphlet and slipped it under the covers. "Hey, guys! Come on in."

"How are you feeling, Regan?" Susan walked in and stood at the foot of the bed.

"Okay, I guess. It's sure great to see you two."

Cynthia paced just inside the door, looking around

the hospital room. Suddenly she stopped and studied Regan. "You don't look that bad."

"How bad am I supposed to look?"

Cynthia said, "You know Becky. She's saying you're not going to die but just be crippled."

"Crippled?" Regan rolled the table away. It crashed against a chair. "Once again, she doesn't know what she's talking about."

"She said you have arthritis and have to use a walker." Susan pointed to the metal stand next to Regan's bed.

"First, they're not sure it's arthritis." Regan whipped back the bedcovers and cautiously moved her legs to the side of the bed. "And second, I only used the walker a couple of days." She slid down the side of the mattress until her feet touched the ground. She willed herself to hide the pain. Standing away from the bed with her hands on her waist, she said, "Give Becky a message for me. Tell her I'm going to be fine. A dancer can't be crippled."

"What about the show tomorrow? Do you think you can do it?" Cynthia looked pointedly at Regan's unstable legs.

"I'm probably going home today—but I'm sure my mom won't let me dance until next week."

"That's okay." Cynthia's posture relaxed. "We'll take care of the show for you. Don't worry about a thing."

"But you don't know the show for this week," Regan said.

"We've already finished the choreography ourselves," Cynthia answered. "But we still need the tape you put together. Mrs. Vigil let us out of school to visit you and get the music for tomorrow's show."

"*You* finished it?"

"Yeah," Cynthia said, "so we need the music."

"Oh—yeah." Regan's mouth soured. The show would go on without her. "Ah—call my mom," she said sadly. "Tell her it's on my desk, next to the computer."

"Great. Okay, we'll see you when you're better." Cynthia turned away.

"Wait! Can't you stay awhile?"

"Can't. Got to run. Feel better," she said over her shoulder.

Susan hesitated. "We really do hope you get better, Regan. I—ah—I guess I'd better go with Cynthia. Bye."

Regan heard Cynthia as they both left the room. "Hospitals give me the willies."

Regan returned to her bed and gingerly pulled herself back onto the sheets.

She wasn't crippled, she wasn't crippled.

She slapped her legs as hard as she could, over and over and over. They were stinging. Finally she began crying. She cried until she fell asleep.

When she awoke an hour later, the pain had lessened and her tears had dried. By midday, the swelling in most of her joints was almost totally gone and her walk close to normal.

The afternoon left little time for her to feel sorry for herself. The physical therapist taught her mother how to help her with some exercises, and they learned new ones for Regan to do on her own. Regan learned about managing her pain with contrast baths, soaking her hand or whatever hurt in cold water, then hot water, then cold and hot again. And they were given stacks of pamphlets to read about juvenile rheumatoid arthritis.

It was obvious what the doctors believed. But it still bothered Regan that the tests couldn't tell her for sure. Maybe the doctors were mistaken. Maybe she had something else.

But right now, this was all the information she had to work with. Regan paid close attention to everything she needed to do. As long as it helped her to keep dancing, she would do whatever she had to.

She and her parents were packing the last of her belongings when Dr. Rich, the pediatric rheumatologist, entered the room. A tall and skinny man with a big bushy mustache, he looked like the push broom they used to sweep the studio floor—except upside down.

"Okay, Regan, review for me our agreement about your going home today."

Regan smiled up at him and said, "Rest for a whole week. No dancing or other activities that would put a strain on my joints."

"Very good. Sounds like you memorized it word for word."

"We'll make sure she follows all your orders, Doctor." Mrs. Shaffer put an arm around her.

"I'm sure you will, and I want you to help her, but the main responsibility for Regan taking care of herself will be her own. You won't be able to be with her all the time."

"Okay, then. How about your medication?" Regan's father questioned her.

"I take three aspirins twice a day. And I'm taking so many I have to eat something when I take them so they don't hurt my stomach." Regan pulled a piece of paper out of her bag. "And I'm supposed to let Mom know if any of this stuff happens to me because it means the amount of aspirin is too much." Regan read, "Rapid or deep breathing, ringing in the ears, vomiting . . ."

Dr. Rich laughed. "Okay, Regan. I'm convinced."

"And don't forget my exercises and eating right. If I do all this, I won't hurt again, and I'll be fine even though you don't really know if I have JRA. Right?"

"I never said you won't hurt again. You're doing very well today, but the pain can come and go. Your tests still don't confirm juvenile rheumatoid arthritis, but your symptoms overwhelmingly point to JRA. It isn't uncommon for the symptoms to be there before the disease is confirmed."

The doctor continued, "For now, we'll try this high-dosage aspirin therapy and watch you very closely. If this doesn't control the inflammation or X rays start showing damage to the joint tissue, we'll have to go to a stronger medication."

Dr. Rich settled onto his heels in front of Regan and looked directly into her eyes. "I'm very impressed with your attention to what you need to do to look after yourself. Just take care of yourself like you've been doing, and you'll be fine. I'll see you in my office next Wednesday."

Regan smiled. She was going home.

"Okay, Mel, so how were they?" Regan lay back in an old recliner chair, drinking hot chocolate with marshmallows. The chair was supposed to have made only a brief stop in the garage on its way to Goodwill more than a year ago. The whole family used it so much for seating in Le Grand Garage Théâtre that it had never made its way to charity.

Mel sat in a folding chair next to her. "How was who?" She lifted a hot, mushy marshmallow out of the mug with her tongue.

"You've been to visit every day for the last five days and haven't mentioned anything about how Cynthia and Susan did with the show last Friday."

"You didn't ask."

"Okay, I'm asking now. How were they?" Regan held her breath.

"All right, I guess. It looked like your stuff but without the—the zing you put to it."

Regan breathed out a sigh of relief.

"So they haven't been by to tell you all about it?" Mel crossed her legs into a pretzel. "Great! I'm glad you told them where to get off."

"No—I didn't." Regan stood up and moved with a slight limp to sit on the edge of the stage. "They're probably just busy doing the show by themselves. I'll see them at school tomorrow."

"You mean you're going to keep seeing them?"

"Mel, I agreed I'd been a jerk to you and apologized, but that didn't mean I'd stop doing things with them. I know this is strange to you, but we've become friends."

"Some friends. If they really were your friends, they would be here cheering you up. What more proof do you need that they're just using you because of the show?"

"They are not. They both came to visit me in the hospital. My being gone must have really thrown them. It's probably taking all of their spare time to get something ready for this week in case I can't do it again."

And that wasn't going to happen, Regan told herself. She'd be ready to dance in two more days. Dr. Rich would give her the all clear later that afternoon, and she'd dance on Friday.

Regan turned toward Mel and spoke softly. "I promise this time I won't let my being friends with them get in the way of our being friends. I promise."

Mel's voice was tight. "Yeah, we'll see."

"How's basketball going? Are you going to win this weekend?" Regan asked.

Mel shook her head. "Whatever am I going to do with you?" Then she smiled. "We're going to kick their slick red shorts!"

Chapter Eighteen

"The doctor really gave you the green light to dance today?" Mel snapped open a lunch-size bag of potato chips. She and Regan were the first ones to claim a prize table in the center of the cafeteria.

"He said I'm fine, and I can dance," Regan answered. "I just have to take the aspirins for a while."

"What about that leg you've been swinging to the side this morning?" Mel pointed toward Regan's right leg. "Your hips are still hurting, aren't they? Do you think you can handle rehearsal today?"

"I can do it," Regan said confidently. "My hips are a little stiff, but I've been working through that."

"Working through it? Regan, you weren't supposed to do anything for a week!"

"I know, I know, but I'm okay. It's almost like none

of this ever happened. The workouts I've been able to sneak in over the last few days have been good."

"Sneak in?" Mel spoke suspiciously. "You mean you've been working out before the doctor's okay, and your parents don't know?"

"It's not a big deal, Mel," Regan defended herself. "It's not unusual for me to dance in my room instead of using the garage."

"But you were told not to."

"It's not like I went out and took a ballet class."

Mel's voice got louder. "Why do you keep trying to hide all this from everyone?"

"I'm not exactly hiding—just doing things on my own," Regan said.

Mel shoved her tray of food to the side. "What do you call not wanting your parents to know when your knee first started hurting? Then you were planning to take the leg splint off so Mrs. Vigil wouldn't know how bad your knee was. Now you're hiding dance workouts from your parents and not following the doctor's orders." Mel leaned across the table and whispered sternly. "I know you want to keep dancing, but you've never lied like this before."

"Lying!" Regan snapped back. "I'm just keeping certain information to myself. That's not lying."

"Well, if it's not, at the very least it's misleading them."

Regan thought for a moment and then spoke again. "Did our parents lie or mislead us when they didn't tell us the Easter Bunny and Santa Claus aren't real?"

"Yes, they did, but only to give us something fun. This is different."

"No, it's not," Regan replied. "I'm not telling certain things so I can do something fun—dance. If my parents had known about my knee from the beginning, I probably wouldn't be host of *Homeroom Exercise* now."

Mel shook her head. "You're just lying by omission."

"If that's what you call it, people do it all the time. How about you?" Regan was angry now. "Have you ever told Becky the truth about how nosy she is, or do you leave out that important piece of information?"

"That's only being kind and you know it."

Regan looked at Mel. "But if you've noticed, I've never 'lied by omission' to you. You know everything."

Mel paused for a minute.

Regan felt hurt. Mel believed she had lied. She *wasn't* lying, she told herself.

Mel looked up at Regan. "It's just that I don't want you to do something stupid and hurt yourself, that's all. Maybe *lie* isn't exactly the right word. I'm sorry I used it. But still—"

"I know you mean well," Regan interrupted her when she saw Cynthia and Susan at the snack bar window. "I'm really okay. Nothing's swollen. I don't have a temperature.

All of this is over, and I don't need to keep things from people anymore. You can stop worrying about me."

Cynthia and Susan, carrying hot dogs and popcorn, walked toward the outside patio door. They must not have seen her. "Cynthia, Susan, over here," Regan called out. "They don't see us." She got up from the table. "Be right back."

"Being invisible does have its upside," Mel said.

Regan glared at Mel.

"What?" Mel answered innocently.

Regan continued across the room and reached the door at the same time as Cynthia and Susan.

"Ah—hi, Regan," Susan said. "Bet you're glad to be out of the hospital."

"You can say that a zillion times twelve."

"You look a little tired, though," Cynthia said, without really looking at her.

"Me, tired? No way. I'm dying to get back to the show. I have it all choreographed. We can pull it together and be ready for the morning. Come on. Mel and I have the center table."

Cynthia took a bite of hot dog. "We're just grabbing something quick," she said.

"We could talk through the order while we eat," Regan answered. "It'll save time this afternoon."

Cynthia reached for the door. "We just can't today. Susan and I've got some stuff to take care of."

"Oh." Regan looked past them through the window to the patio. Some of Cynthia's friends were gathered around a picnic table. "I guess I'll see you at rehearsal, then."

"Yeah. Come on, Susan." The two girls disappeared through the door.

For a moment, Regan watched them join the girls at the table. Then she went back to Mel.

"So, the fashion police didn't want to sit with me?" Mel questioned. "Thank goodness for small favors."

Maybe that was it—they just didn't want to sit with Mel. "They had . . . things they had to do." She stuffed her sandwich and apple into her lunch bag. "Let's get out of here. I'm not very hungry."

By the end of the day, Regan was tired, although she moved toward her locker relatively pain free. But she hadn't been able to concentrate that afternoon. All she could think about was Mel saying she had lied.

Was it really lying? No one had asked her a direct question to which she had purposely given the wrong answer. That was lying. All Regan had been doing this year was protecting her opportunities to dance. She'd *had* to keep certain information to herself, that was all.

And she wasn't being deceitful. She wasn't trying to hurt anyone. She just wanted to dance.

She felt confused. She didn't know what she believed anymore.

"Regan," a voice called to her. "Regan, just the person I wanted to see," Mrs. Vigil said as she came out of the principal's office.

"Hi, Mrs. Vigil."

"How are you? We've all been so worried about you." Mrs. Vigil put an arm around her shoulders and walked her toward a bench.

"I'm doing okay. But it's great to be back at school. Staying at home was about to drive me crazy."

"But rest is necessary for your recovery. Are you in much pain?"

"No, I'm just kind of stiff sometimes."

"You do look a bit pale."

"I'll be fine. I'll just need some rest after rehearsal. But I've got some great ideas for the show tomorrow."

Mrs. Vigil turned toward her. "That's what I wanted to talk to you about. I think you're jumping back into all your activities too fast. Maybe we should let Cynthia and Susan do the show for a bit, while you get your strength back."

"*Without me?* But my doctor said I could dance."

"It will just be temporary, until you're stronger. I can see you're not feeling your best yet. I don't want you jeopardizing your health or your future as a dancer."

"But I'm—"

"What I was thinking," Mrs. Vigil persisted, "is that you could write a dance column for the school newspaper while you rest for a few more weeks. You could review dance performances, put in exercise tips, that sort of thing."

"Really, Mrs. Vigil, the dance column sounds great, but I'm fine. My doctor's not worried. I've completely recovered. See." She stood up and barreled into the jazz routine she'd been planning for that week.

"Careful, Regan."

She stopped just short of hitting the wall at the end of a series of leap turns that finished in a sliding split. All in complete control. A little winded, Regan said, "Does it look like I can't continue as the host of *Homeroom Exercise*?"

Mrs. Vigil chuckled. "Regan, you win. You seem to be in top shape." She helped Regan off the floor. "You just tell Cynthia you feel fine and we'll keep things as they are, but let me know if you need a rest. Your health is more important than this show."

"Don't worry, Mrs. Vigil. I'd better get going." Regan trotted down the hall, waving behind her. "Thanks."

She got to her locker and rotated the knob on her combination lock. Ten—two—sixteen.

"Hi, Regan, hi! I've been trying to talk to you all day. How are you? Look at you standing and walking and everything, who would think?" Becky slid to a halt next to Regan's locker, dropping two books off the top of the pile she carried in her arms.

Becky spoke while trying to retrieve her books. "Say, I can't believe Cynthia talked Mrs. Vigil into letting her and Susan take over *Homeroom Exercise* from you. You look okay to me."

Regan froze. "What did you say?"

"Cynthia and Susan. It's a shame about them taking the show from you."

"Becky, stop it—just stop it. Quit being a busybody trying to play with everyone's lives." Regan pulled her exercise clothes out of her locker and slammed the door.

"Really, Regan, it's true."

"Yeah, sure, like when you told everyone I might die. This last time you had me crippled in a wheelchair for the rest of my life. Now you're trying to make me hate my friends."

Regan closed her eyes, holding her fists against her mouth. Then she opened her hands and held them tautly against her cheeks. "Just—stay—out—of—my—life." She punched each word.

Regan turned and walked away. Her body shook. Her chest heaved. She could feel anger crawling from her stomach into her chest. It burned.

"Regan—Regan! You've heard, haven't you?" It was Mel.

"That dirty snake. Even *I* didn't think she'd go so low as to get you off the show completely."

Regan found her voice. "Has Becky already gotten to you, too? You know she's a liar—really and truly a liar, not that 'lying by omission' stuff."

"I didn't get this from Becky. Mrs. Vigil told me after fourth period."

"Mrs. Vigil? Just exactly what . . . what did she say?"

Mel let out a deep breath. "Basically, that Cynthia came to her and said you were too sick to do the show and that Cynthia and Susan would host it alone for a few weeks so you can rest. It was clear the idea didn't originate with Mrs. Vigil—it was Cynthia's idea."

"Cynthia hasn't even seen me in a week!" Regan twisted her leotard and tights with her hands as if she were trying to snap them in two. Mel wouldn't lie to her. It had to be true. So that's what Mrs. Vigil meant when she said to tell Cynthia she felt fine.

No wonder Cynthia hadn't wanted to sit with her at lunch. She had already convinced Mrs. Vigil to give her the show. She had known right then, right at that moment, and hadn't said a word.

Regan brushed past Mel into the hallway of the gym where a boom box blared a song Regan hated. Cynthia and Susan moved through a jazz combination.

Regan stood in the middle of the hall, forcing her arms rigid against her sides. Her pounding heart would make a dent inside her chest if it didn't slow down.

The music stopped.

Cynthia turned to Regan. Her eyebrows rose. Her lips curled into a triumphant sneer. "Don't you think you should go home and rest, Regan?"

"It didn't work." Regan tried to control her shaking voice.

"Of course it did," Cynthia stated.

"You can just pack up your music and bad choreography and get out," Regan ordered.

Cynthia stood dead still. "I've had enough of you, Regan. I'm sick and tired of listening to everyone say how good you are and how humble you are. But I know the truth. You're not as good as you think you are."

Regan froze. That was exactly what she'd always thought about Cynthia. What Regan had always thought about herself was, Was she as good as people said? What was the reality? One person's truth could be another person's lie.

"Staring at me with your mouth open is *so* attractive, Regan."

Regan swallowed.

"Just step aside like a good little girl," Cynthia said.

"I'm not going anywhere." Regan felt sweat trickle down her back. "I'm perfectly capable of doing the show. Mrs. Vigil's not making any changes."

"I don't believe you."

"Go ask her yourself. I just talked to her ten minutes ago. Then Mel told me what you did. You probably had this planned all along."

Susan went to her dance bag. "Cynthia, I told you. I told you it was a bad idea."

"It only turned out bad because Regan's Mrs. Vigil's pet. We'll see about this." Cynthia picked up her towel and threw it around her neck. "You've always been such a loser, Regan. You're never going to dance with the New York City Ballet company, never in Hollywood— even the local rinky-dink companies won't touch you."

Regan struggled to keep control. "Get *out* of here."

"With pleasure." Cynthia sauntered over to her CD player near the wall and slowly picked it up.

Regan's insides boiled. "I am *not* a loser. But I was temporarily blind about you."

"From the way Becky tells it, crippled is more likely."

Regan lunged for Cynthia, but Mel suddenly appeared between them. "That's enough, you guys."

Regan turned and ran out of the gym a split second before the others could see her cry.

Chapter Nineteen

Regan didn't deserve to be a prima ballerina, because she was a prima idiot. How could she have believed Cynthia was her friend? She felt so embarrassed for being fooled.

But her embarrassment didn't erase her anger. It only grew stronger the next morning when she walked into the DVTV studio. She knew she had to be hallucinating. Cynthia, Susan, and Mrs. Vigil were sitting around a small table, drinking tea.

"I can't believe you two are here. You don't actually think you're doing the show with me today, or ever again for that matter," Regan shouted.

"Easy now, Regan." Mrs. Vigil put down her Styrofoam cup and guided Regan to the table where the three of them sat. "It's obvious, Regan, that you and

Cynthia have a problem you need to work out, but I'd like to hear your side of the story."

"I'm not the one with the problem, Mrs. Vigil. Cynthia's the one that's been scheming to take the show away from me. She planned it from the day she lost the first audition. Just what did she tell you?"

Regan watched Cynthia look at Mrs. Vigil with sad eyes. They even glistened with tears. What an actress!

"We do have two stories here," Mrs. Vigil said. "Cynthia claims she wasn't trying to take your place and that she was just concerned about your health."

"My health! If you want me to have backup dancers, fine, but please choose two other people. It's not fair to let these back stabbers represent the school to the whole city."

Susan squirmed uncomfortably in her chair.

Mrs. Vigil replied, "The only decision I'm going to make for the two of you is the one that affects the show and our school. It's too late to get new dancers and train them before the first citywide show next Friday, and it's definitely too late for this morning's show."

"But they don't know today's show," Regan stated firmly. "I can do it without them."

Mrs. Vigil shook her head. "They can follow. They know your style. After that, Regan and Cynthia, let me know how you solve your problem. Your only guideline is the solution cannot inconvenience or hurt another person."

Mrs. Vigil shifted her gaze to Cynthia and held it there long and steady. Then, without another word, she left.

Cynthia's sad cow eyes turned dark, and a smirk grew on her face. "You didn't think we were going to just quit and let you go citywide without us?" She flipped her hair behind her shoulders. "Mrs. Vigil always has such a sense of fair play."

Regan still held her dance bag on her shoulder, and the leather strap squeaked under her tight, torturous grip. A twinge flared through her left elbow. "The only way for us to solve our problem is for you to get lost," Regan said.

"Won't happen, little ballerina," Cynthia stated. "I'm here for the ride."

Regan took a deep breath. "You still don't think Mrs. Vigil has you figured out, do you? I'll tell you this, Cynthia, if she doesn't know now, *I'll* make sure she does."

The big day of the first citywide *Homeroom Exercise* show finally arrived, but the week getting there was tough. Cynthia and Susan showed up for rehearsal every afternoon. Cynthia harassed Regan more than she rehearsed. She made fun of every dance step and exercise Regan put in the show. Susan tried to rehearse, but Cynthia made it impossible. Most of the time the pair sat around eating Chee-tos and drinking Cokes.

After two days of that, Regan thought of a way to fix Cynthia for good. It was the least Cynthia deserved for trying to steal the show from her.

Regan loved her plan. The show she rehearsed at school would not be the one she would dance on Friday. At home she secretly choreographed another show—different music, different steps, different formations.

This was the first secret she'd kept from Mel, and it made Regan uncomfortable. But after their discussion the previous week on lying and deceit, she couldn't be sure what Mel would think of her plan.

Cynthia and Susan would be laughed at in middle schools all over town for being incompetent fools. The pleasure of this revenge radiated through Regan's entire body like a good workout.

Unfortunately, Regan's good feelings didn't make up for what she felt physically. She'd been feverish on and off during the week. Food didn't look good to her. She told her mom she couldn't eat because of nerves. But she knew it was happening again. Her knees and elbows were puffy, and the pain in her hands made it difficult to open the aspirin bottle.

But she had hidden her symptoms well and now stood in a small studio at the PBS station waiting to be on real television for the first time in her dancing career. This could mean so much to her. A video producer might be a guest speaker at one of the schools and see the show. Then he'd ask who she was, and the rest would be history.

Regan sat at one of the dressing tables against the front wall of the TV studio with Mel's lucky key chain in her hand. She smiled at herself in the mirror outlined in big round lightbulbs. Being here was great. Even better still was that Cynthia and Susan hadn't shown up yet. Maybe they had chickened out. But then her plan to embarrass them in front of the whole city wouldn't work.

That might be best. The decision made for her. She had been wavering on whether to do it or not. Regan wanted so much to put Cynthia in her place. But each day during the week, she thought a little clearer and realized messing them up could make her look bad. And if she did switch the tapes, that made her as deceitful as Cynthia. But Regan wanted to hurt Cynthia. She deserved it.

Regan put Mel's key chain back in her bag and looked at the two music tapes on the table. She pulled her thick hair into a ponytail with a hot pink tie that matched the stripe across the front of her leotard.

Cynthia and Susan, if they showed, would wear the same leotard except in navy.

She slid off the director's chair at the dressing table and turned to admire the set again. It was so cool. The TV station had built three round platforms for the exercise part of the program. Their names, outlined in glitter, decorated the front of each one. Regan's platform sat in front of the other two. Cynthia's and Susan's platforms could easily be removed if they didn't show up.

Whack! A hand pounded Regan's back. "Daydreaming about your fame, are you?" Cynthia said as she and Susan walked past her and sat at the next two sets of mirrors.

They had showed. Now she would have to make a decision.

Regan picked up the tapes and got three aspirins, then two more, out of her dance bag. "A little late, aren't we?" she questioned. She went to the water fountain by the door and choked down the aspirins. They stuck in her throat even with the help of the water. She took the aspirins, including the two extras, an hour early, but she needed them.

"Light check," one of the technicians called. A bank of yellow lights at the back of the set lit up. "Lights, stage right." A group of blue and red lights on a pole flashed onto the set.

It was real. It was really happening. Her palms sweated.

Cynthia and Susan primped at the mirrors.

"Get with it, you two. You better do some warming up, or you'll make fools of yourselves. We start soon."

"Yes, Mommy," Cynthia whined like a three-year-old.

Regan was already warmed up, had been to the bathroom three times, and felt like she had to go again. She wanted to get started so that her nervousness would go away.

"Your music, please, Regan," the technician called.

Regan walked over to him, holding a tape in each hand. She looked from one to the other. She saw in her mind Mel's face, then her mother's face, then her father's. She took a deep breath and handed him a tape.

"Places, ladies!" the director bellowed.

Regan inched toward the set. The muscles in her hips throbbed and her hands quivered. She never remembered feeling this nervous for anything in her life. But she knew it would go away once she started dancing.

She stood on her platform, shaking her hands. The heat from the stage lights penetrated her skin. Cynthia and Susan whispered behind her on their platforms. Cynthia's voice came through. "Don't make a mistake, Regan. The whole world's watching."

The director counted down the seconds to airtime. On each count he pointed to Regan. "Four, three, two—" He didn't call out the number one. He only pointed one finger at Regan and then her music and introduction started. "Welcome to *Homeroom Exercise*! The weekly exercise show for middle school students, presented by middle school students. Your host for *Homeroom Exercise*—Regan Shaffer!"

The music—for the show she had rehearsed with Cynthia and Susan during the week—rang out around them. Regan relaxed. Cynthia and Susan didn't know how close they had come to total humiliation.

The music continued, and their opening exercises smoothly transitioned into step touches while she briefly explained what she wanted the students to do.

She led students through a warm-up, then into the low-impact aerobic section. Everything went as planned, but her jitters didn't disappear as they normally did. She continued to tremble, and sweat seeped from her pores.

The routine moved into a kicking section. Regan felt like she wore ankle weights designed for elephants. She could hardly lift her legs to kick. Pain tore at her hips. The arthritis was back. But she would not stop.

It was time for the jazz combination. The three of them pushed their platforms off to the side to make room. Cynthia whispered to Regan as they passed, "What's wrong with you? And you were worried about *us* doing a good job."

Regan said nothing. Instead, she willed herself into the start of the jazz combination. Each movement radiated excruciating pain.

She pounced into the preparation for a big jump and sprung her body up into the air with her legs in a wide split. The jump was beauty and pain coexisting. The landing was ghastly, and the end of a dream.

Her knees collapsed, and she fell forward on her face.

Chapter Twenty

Regan landed facing a TV monitor on the right-hand corner of the set. She watched the images of herself and of the chaos her collapse created.

The music continued. Cynthia and Susan stood behind her looking helpless. Then two men passed in front of the camera, momentarily blocking everything on the screen. Next Regan found herself watching the preview of a symphony concert to be broadcast on the PBS station.

Someone spoke to her. "Dear, did you break something?"

"No—nothing's broken." Regan made an attempt to roll from her stomach to her side.

"Don't move. Don't move until the paramedics get here."

*　　　*　　　*

At the hospital, Regan quietly submitted her body and will to the care of the nurses and staff. She answered when necessary but spoke little to her mother, father, or Mel. She had nothing to say. Emotional pain, as well as physical pain, wrapped around her body and soul.

Mindlessly, she endured the hospital routine: pain medication, hot and cold treatments, the big hot-water mattress, falling in and out of exhausted sleep. The day and much of the pain passed.

The next morning, Regan woke to see her mother sitting in the chair next to her hospital bed. She looked so scared and worried. Regan reached for her and broke into tears. Regan's voice shook. "It wasn't supposed to happen again."

Regan's mother rocked her in her arms. "You're going to be okay, baby. You're going to be fine. You're better now. The pain medication is working."

"I did everything Dr. Rich told me. What happened? What did I do wrong?"

"Regan, sweetheart, having this disease is not your fault. You didn't do anything wrong to deserve JRA." She stroked Regan's forehead with her hand. "I've been trying all night long to make sense of this. I can't."

Her mother's thumb traced small circles at Regan's temple. "You know, Regan—some kids wear glasses, some kids get diabetes, some break their legs. Everybody has something in their life that doesn't make it perfect. You have arthritis. I know how you like to plan everything just so and this doesn't fit your plan, but it isn't something you can control."

Regan cried in her mother's arms until her breaths came in hiccuping gasps.

The door opened, and her father and Dr. Rich entered.

Mr. Shaffer kissed her cheek. "Hi, Twinkle Toes."

She burst into tears again.

"Oh, Regan, I'm sorry." He looked into her eyes and gently dried her tears with the back of his fingers.

Dr. Rich stood at the foot of her bed. "How's your pain today?"

"Better," she said quietly.

"They tell me your fever broke around midnight and the swelling has improved. Let's take a look." Dr. Rich examined her knees, ankles, elbows, and hands and seemed satisfied.

He adjusted the sheets back over her legs and stood looking down at her. "Regan, your test results finally confirm it. You have juvenile rheumatoid arthritis."

A renewed surge of pain washed over her body. Her eyes quickly pooled with tears again. "Will I . . . will I be crippled?"

"No, Regan, no." Dr. Rich shook his head. "The chances of that happening are very slim."

Lana Shaffer placed her hands on Regan's—a layer of warmth over bitter cold.

Dr. Rich rolled a stool up to Regan's bed and sat close to her. "Regan, arthritis doesn't always end up as a crippling disease. It's different from an adult getting rheumatoid arthritis. Most children with arthritis live a fairly normal life and go into adulthood with very little permanent damage."

A tear escaped and rolled down her cheek.

"I've seen that you're a very strong and determined young lady. Use that drive to take care of yourself within the constraints of the disease, and you'll manage fine."

"Fine!" Regan yelled at the doctor. "How can I ever be fine again if I can't dance?" Tears streamed down her face. "Can you tell me I'll be able to dance?"

"Regan, calm down," her father said quietly.

Dr. Rich held up his hand to Mr. Shaffer. "No—no—it's all right. This is a lot for Regan to take in." He looked at her. "You should be able to dance. I encourage you to try. It will be a good form of exercise along with your physical therapy." He put his hand on her forearm. "But I'm going to be honest with you. You'll have good days and bad. When the inflammation is severe, you'll need to rest. Other days, you can dance."

Regan made no attempt to dry her eyes.

"Dr. Rich, what about the treatment?" her father questioned. "What do we do now?"

Dr. Rich clasped his hands together. "First of all we've got to get this inflammation under control so that we can put an end to these flares. The aspirin's not cutting it. We need to go to a stronger nonsteroidal anti-inflammatory drug. There are a variety to choose from, and we may have to try a few before we find the one that works best for Regan."

Regan looked at the doctor, then leaned exhaustedly back into her mother's arms.

"Once again," Dr. Rich said to her, "the physical therapy is important to keep any loss to your range of motion at a minimum. I've scheduled you to see the physical therapist this afternoon. Besides working with you on . . ."

Dr. Rich and her parents continued to talk. But Regan couldn't listen anymore.

It didn't look as if positive thinking and working through the pain, as she had always done with her dancing, would work for this. She was no longer in control. Her body had betrayed her.

The physical therapist showed up with a wheelchair to take her to P.T. Dan was the biggest man Regan had ever seen close up—not fat big, but tall with muscles. She obediently let him help her into the chair and wheel her away to the physical therapy room. Everyone kept saying physical therapy would help—she would have to try.

The warm water of the hydrotherapy tub melted away some of the tension as well as the pain. But that vacation from pain was short-lived. She lay on a padded table, dressed in a loose warm-up outfit. Dan slowly moved her bent right knee up toward her chest. He got it about three-quarters of the way there and stopped.

"It can go farther. You can push it all the way to my chest."

"Not by the grimace on your face, I can't. First rule, Regan: Learn the difference between a normal muscle-stretching pain and a joint-arthritic pain. Now, you being a dancer as they've told me, you have an advantage over some people. Some people don't know their bodies at all."

Dan gently moved her knee to the side toward the table. "When you feel the arthritis pain, stop. Don't go any farther. I hear you're some great jazz dancer. Personally, I prefer watching ballet. Ballet takes as much discipline and focus as physical therapy does." He returned the right leg to its starting position and picked up the left.

Regan looked up at Dan. "I never thought of it that—ouch."

"Ah, sorry. See, now, that was too far. Okay, let's sit you up." Dan helped her into a sitting position on the table. "Now I want you to lift your right thigh off the table as far as is comfortable."

How easy, Regan thought. She lifted her right knee. At least she tried. It felt like picking up what you thought was an empty box and finding it full of bowling balls. She grasped the side of the table with her hands and tried again as best as she could with the pain. Her knee lifted about an inch.

"Relax, take it easy. The strength will come. You'll be amazed after a while when the medication reduces the swelling. Try again. Just a small lift. Exhale when you lift."

Regan looked over Dan's shoulder as she exhaled and lifted her knee. A boy who looked a couple of years younger than her lifted himself out of a wheelchair. With the help of a therapist, he stood between two long horizontal bars. The equipment looked like gymnastic parallel bars, except lower.

He wore braces with leather straps and a metal ring at the knee. The braces trapped his legs from thighs to shins. Holding on to the bars on each side of him, the boy slowly shuffled along in a pitiful walk. Each step was only a couple of inches. Regan saw the pain in his face and felt the pain in her hips with each step he took and each lift of her knee.

"What's wrong with him?" She gestured with her head toward the boy.

Dan turned to look. "You know, everyone in here is an individual, and you all have different circumstances.

Diseases affect people to varying degrees." He looked back at Regan. "Chase also has polyarticular arthritis. Just like you, most of his joints are involved. But he's had it since he was four years old, and he has just had surgery on his knees. When he's old enough, he may have to have some of his joints replaced. Yours won't get to that point."

Regan closed her eyes.

"Now, listen to me. You and the doctors caught this fairly early. With proper care and medication, that's not going to happen to you. And proper care includes these exercises. Let's get back to work."

Dan kept her facing away from the boy with the braces and guided her through the rest of the exercises. Regan said nothing the rest of the session.

Back in her hospital room, Dan helped her into bed and arranged the sheets. "You're going to beat this. I know you can. Dancers have a lot of strength. I'll be back to get you in the morning."

How could she beat something like this? How could she ever find enough strength?

She spotted something new on the bedside table. It was her dance journal. Her mother must have put it there when she was out of the room.

Regan stared at the journal for a long time. Finally she picked it up. She turned the pages one at a time, looking at quotes. She stopped at one by Eugene Gilson and read in a whisper:

"It is not enough to want to be a dancer in order to be able to become one. Here the body has the first and final word."

She closed her eyes and saw her familiar ballet studio. There she was, dancing in all her splendor—braces engulfing her legs and arms, clunking as she stumbled through pirouettes and jetés, and crashing together as she fell down. People laughed. Pain stabbed through her imperfect body.

She opened her eyes and rummaged through the journal until she found her list, "Career in Dance." Regan ripped out the page and crumpled it into a ball. It would make a nice little fire.

Chapter Twenty-one

Plastic covered everything—the grapefruit, the oat-meal, the small glass of milk. After sitting untouched for two hours, the oatmeal was dry, cracked, and bumpy, like a face ravaged by years of acne.

She sat with her arms crossed over her chest and stared beyond her breakfast tray to the corner of the ceiling. She imagined the paint peeling, ever so slowly, from the wall.

"Morning, sweetheart." Her mother entered her hospital room and went to the side of her bed. "How did you sleep last night? Here, let me help you with your breakfast." Mrs. Shaffer peeled the plastic wrap off each breakfast item. "How long has this been sitting here?"

"Awhile, I guess."

"We'll have to get you another tray. Why didn't you eat when they brought it to you?"

Regan's eyes dropped down to the thin white sheets. "I wasn't hungry."

A knock came from the doorway. "Knock, knock. Good morning, ladies. How's my dancer today?" Dan boomed into the room steering a wheelchair tipped back on its hind wheels. "Next stop, physical therapy."

"Regan, do you want me to get you another breakfast before you go or do you want to wait for lunch?"

Regan didn't reply. She just continued to stare at the sheets.

"Regan?" Mrs. Shaffer moved the rollaway table aside and carefully sat next to Regan on the bed. "What is it?"

Regan whispered, "I'm not going."

"Not going—to physical therapy?" Her mother looked back at Dan. "Is it too painful?"

"She did great yesterday. No problems."

Regan turned away from her mother onto her aching hips. That all-too-familiar feeling of tears building burned behind her eyes.

Dan sat in the wheelchair. "I know yesterday wasn't easy, but this is the best way for you to get better. You're a smart girl; you know you've got to do this."

Mrs. Shaffer tried to hug her. "Come on, I'll go with you."

Regan pulled away. "No," she screamed. "I'm not going. There's no use. I'm going to be crippled. I'm not going to be able to dance." She buried her face into the pillow and sobbed.

"Dan? Do you know what this is all about?" her mother asked.

"I have an idea," Dan answered. "She saw a boy with JRA in the therapy room yesterday. He's recovering from knee surgery and wears braces to walk."

"I see," she said slowly.

The two of them tried to convince her she wouldn't be crippled. No matter what they said, they couldn't put a dent in her belief that she would end up like the boy with the braces. She refused to go to therapy, tuned everyone out, and nightly dreamed about fumbling around in braces.

On Tuesday, after four days in the hospital, she went home. That first day she wouldn't even come out of her room for meals. The second day, Mr. Shaffer carried her to the living room and sat her on the couch.

"You've got to have a change of scenery, Regan," he said. "You haven't even been in your garage theater since you've been home."

"No point," she almost whispered.

"At least today you can sit here and watch me repot this root-bound ficus tree."

Saying nothing, she watched him work. First he pruned the branches of the leafy tree down to stubs. Then he grabbed the tree by its trunk and yanked it out of the pot. Regan grimaced as he deftly sliced half the root ball off with a gleaming kitchen knife. Her dad repotted the tree with fresh soil and water, then hid it in a back corner behind the healthy plants.

That's what had happened to her, Regan thought. She'd been stripped of her beautiful limbs and should hide in a corner. But she'd never get the fresh soil and water the ficus received. She was crippled and there was nothing she could do about it.

After she watched him repot the ficus, Regan's father couldn't get her out of her room again. She refused to do her physical therapy exercises. She picked at the food her mother brought on a tray. She just sat. She had no desire to do anything.

She especially didn't want to see Becky when she arrived on Wednesday afternoon.

Regan was lying facedown on her bed when she heard the bedroom door open. No one had knocked. She didn't look up until she heard a voice.

"Regan?" Becky said meekly. "Are you awake?"

Becky. She couldn't believe it. "Becky, what are you doing here?"

"I—I—I just wanted to tell you how sorry I am that you're sick." Becky inched into the room. "And I wanted to tell you something else."

Regan sighed. She rolled over and pushed herself up into a sitting position. "That's nice, Becky, but you didn't have to come. I just need to rest and be alone, so if you'd please, just go."

"Regan, please, I have to say this." Becky took a deep breath. "You were right when you called me a busybody and all that other stuff. I'm sorry I told people you had cancer, it's just that I heard my mom talking and she said—"

"I know, I know." Regan interrupted Becky before she went on and on. "It doesn't matter anymore," she said. "It might as well be cancer. Don't worry about it."

For the first time Regan could remember, Becky said nothing.

A remorseful Becky was worse than a clueless one. "You know, Becky," Regan began, "I'm sorry I lost my temper and said all those things. At least that time, about Cynthia and the show, you were right."

Becky perked up. "That really was mean of Cynthia, and now we know what she's like, don't we?"

"Look, Becky, thanks for coming, but I'm tired, and I just want to be alone."

"Okay, Regan," Becky answered. "I hope you get to dance again real soon." She bopped out of the room.

Thursday afternoon, her mom tried to get her to watch the *Cinderella* ballet on PBS. "You love that ballet," her mom said. "After you watch, you could write a review for the school newspaper. Isn't that what you told me Mrs. Vigil said you could do?"

She didn't answer. She turned in her bed to face the wall.

Her mom sat on the bed and rubbed her back. They stayed quiet that way for a long time. Finally her mom kissed the back of her head and left the room.

That evening Regan tossed in her sleep, and the pain in her hips bolted her awake. She reached for a sip of water from the glass by her bed. Her hand muscles gripped to hold it, but as she lifted, a spasm caused her to slosh water onto the carpet. "Awww . . ." she moaned. She used two hands to place the glass back on the table, lay back, closed her eyes, and tried to sleep again.

But her mind started dancing. It danced her studio's production of *Cinderella.* She relived standing in the wings at the theater, watching the older dancers balancing and twirling with ease. Then her part came. She and her classmates were the court dancers. They danced behind Cinderella and the prince and got to be on stage when Cinderella lost her slipper and jumped into the coach before it turned back into a pumpkin. Regan loved the pumpkin coach. It actually had wheels and moved across the stage.

She turned on the light and got out of bed. Regan's bare feet recoiled as she stepped on a spot of cold, wet carpet. She hobbled to her closet and dug to the back until she found her court dancer's costume.

It was her favorite. The bright pink tutu was the fullest grown-up tutu she ever had. The bodice was sequined, and chiffon draped over her shoulders. The best part was the pink sequined tiara.

She hung the costume on the closet door and took the tiara to her dressing table. She sat down, put her hair up in a bun, and pinned the tiara in place. Then she closed her eyes, hummed her music, and fantasized through the *Cinderella* dance.

She stood, determined to dance. Her first step into a waltz turn burned her knee and her thigh muscles quivered. She moved forward in relevé two steps and faltered—too weak to continue. One tear trickled down her cheek to her chin. She began, ever so slowly, to spin in circles—round and round. Just as slowly, a haunted whisper came from her mouth. "Row—row—row, your boat, gently down the stream; merrily, merrily, merrily, merrily—dance—is but a dream." She melted to the floor, sobbing.

Not until she was cried out and exhausted did she fall asleep in her bed.

Two hours later, her father came into her room. "Regan, wake up."

Regan threw her arms over her eyes in protection against the bright April sunlight her father invited into her room when he lifted the shades. "Ohhh, Dad."

Regan groaned and turned her face into the pillow, knocking the sequined tiara from her head.

"Come on, Regan, you've got to get up. We've talked to Dr. Rich, and he said your rest week is over. It's time you get back to school."

"How can I possibly get around at school? Can't Mom get my work, and I'll do it at home?"

Regan felt the mattress give slightly as her father sat on the foot of her bed. "Your walking is fine, and Dr. Rich said the medication brought down most of the swelling before you left the hospital. He also said you'd be feeling a little more comfortable if you'd do your exercises. This lying around is just making you weak and stiff."

"Dad, I'm not ready." She turned over onto her back and pulled the covers up around her neck.

"You need to get ready. Your mother and I won't insist on you going today, but by Monday, you need to get back."

He stood up and looked at her droopy fuchsia plant on the bureau. "You haven't even watered this poor plant. I'll get a pitcher and water it before it dies."

Regan shouted, "No—leave it. I want it to die."

Her father froze. "You're scaring me, Regan." He moved closer to her and picked up the tiara that was wedged between her pillow and the headboard. "We've tried helping you with this, giving you your own time to accept this disease and deal with it. Nothing seems to be working. If you can't get a hold of yourself by Monday, we're going to need outside help."

He kissed her forehead. "I love you, Regan." Then he turned and placed the tiara on her dressing table. "I'll see you when I get home tonight."

Outside help? What did he mean, a shrink? She wasn't crazy. She just didn't see the point anymore. What her father said when she was in the hospital that first time, when they thought she was asleep—he was right. She'd lost her dream. Her heart was beating, but never again would she be truly alive. A heavy weariness drifted down her face. She turned over and slept.

Regan's mom let her sleep most of the day, but going back to school became the main topic of conversation when her mother caught her awake. Even Mel jumped right in as soon as she showed up after school.

"Hey, what's going on with you? I know you're scared. But you really lied this time—and to me! You told me the doctor said you had to stay home this week and do nothing. But your mom just told me it's okay for you to go back to school. *And* you're supposed to be doing your therapy."

"Don't you start on me, too," she shot at Mel. "I don't care what I said. I don't care about anything."

"That's abundantly obvious. Not only can't you get to school, you're not even dressed again today. You're starting to smell like sweaty tights left in a dance bag for a week."

"Sorry my odor offends you." Regan sat leaning against the wall. "I just can't see any reason to get dressed—or to go back to school—ever."

"Besides it being the law and you needing an education so you don't end up in the poorhouse, as my dad would say, there's me. I miss you."

"I can't go back and face all those kids. I've made a total fool of myself—not just to the kids at Desert Vista but to everyone in the whole city."

"Look, you," Mel said, "nobody cares that you fell. They know what's wrong with you, and that you aren't just a klutz."

Regan snapped, "So they know I'm crippled. See what I mean? There's no reason to go back to school. I've lost my show. Cynthia has turned out to be scum. I can't dance anymore. What's the point in even getting up in the morning?"

Mel lost it. "Really feeling sorry for yourself aren't you? There are worse things than arthritis."

Regan glared at Mel. "Like what?"

Mel spoke slowly. "You have a short memory. Like leukemia, for example."

Regan studied her thumbnail.

"Your mom told me what the doctor said—that

there's almost no chance that you'll get so bad you can't walk or dance."

"You didn't see the boy who has JRA. He may even have his joints replaced!"

"She told me about him, too, and that it's not going to happen to you." Mel paced the room. "Even if it did, there are things you can do connected with dance other than actually dancing. You can write about dance or choreograph."

"I'm supposed to be a dancer, Mel. And dancers dance. They don't sit in a chair and tell others how to do it."

"Well, that may be your only choice if you don't get off your butt, do your exercises, and take care of yourself."

"It's not that easy," Regan whispered.

"What was that?" Mel stopped pacing.

Regan shouted, "It's not that easy!"

"So what else is new? You've never given up before. You may have to work a little harder, but you can do it."

Mel sat down in front of Regan. "You've always worked hard—for everything. You've even become a school celebrity—although an unfortunate by-product of that popularity is Cynthia and Susan."

Regan looked Mel in the eye. "Now there, I agree with you. I really let myself get taken in."

"I do have good news for you on that subject." Mel's lips curved into a mischievous grin.

"What?" Regan straightened her back, interested in something for the first time in a week.

"Cynthia dug her own grave." Mel spoke with satisfaction. "After school yesterday, Mrs. Vigil asked me to find a notebook she'd left in the TV studio. When I got there, the species Cynthius-e-Susius were lounging around, gossiping, and drinking Cokes."

"I bet Cynthia couldn't contain her excitement about my most recent demise," Regan said.

"That's an understatement, Regan. She was going on and on about how good they were going to be as the permanent hosts. I was just leaving before I got into a fight with them when something happened."

"What?"

"Cynthia and Susan had their backs to the door of the studio, and I was facing it. Cynthia was right in the middle of saying Mrs. Vigil was a fool for choosing you to be host, when guess who appeared in the doorway?"

"Mrs. Vigil?" Regan guessed hopefully.

"Mrs. Vigil," Mel repeated. "She just stood there, with her arms crossed, listening. I did ask Cynthia a few leading questions to make sure Mrs. Vigil heard about everything, but mostly, Cynthia sabotaged herself."

Mel continued, "She bragged about making friends with you so you would want them as the backup dancers. Then she told me about telling Mrs. Vigil you were too sick to dance so she could get the show for herself. Cynthia loves to talk, and she confessed it all."

Regan put her hand to her mouth and lightly gasped. "I wish I could have seen Mrs. Vigil's face when she heard."

"You know, she didn't look that surprised," Mel said. "All she said was, 'Usually when I give someone trust and an opportunity to grow, they rise to the occasion. If I were in your place, I would feel very disappointed with myself, Cynthia.' Then she left the room."

Mel's smile broadened, and her eyes sparkled. "But today I found out Cynthia's off the show, *and* suspended for two days, *and* has to do community service. All Mrs. Vigil did to Susan was take her off the show and have a long talk with her."

Regan clapped her hands. "You are the most beautiful friend in the whole world. I could kiss you." She reached out and pecked Mel on the cheek with a smacking sound.

Mel laughed.

"So if Cynthia and Susan aren't doing the show, who is?"

"Since it's getting kind of close to the end of the year, Mrs. Vigil decided to cancel it completely. She said she'd have to wait until fall to consider it again."

"I don't know why that should make me sadder than I am. I've already lost all my opportunities now that I'm crippled."

Mel tipped back to her heels and shrieked, "You're not going to be crippled. Stop it!" She stood up and put her hands on her hips. "Look, just get up and get dressed."

"I can't."

"Stop feeling sorry for yourself, Regan! You make me so mad!"

Mel headed for the door but turned before she got there. "*I'm* not giving up. I'll be back." She slammed the door behind her.

Chapter Twenty-two

Regan managed to take a shower by the time Mel arrived early the following afternoon. Her hair hung uncurled, and she wore an old pair of jeans with the knees busted out and a white T-shirt. It might not be as much as Mel wanted from her, but at least she was clean.

Regan loosely pulled the sheets up on her bed and sat there looking out the window at the spring afternoon. In the distance, she could see the cables of the tramcars on the mountain glistening in the sun. Just below her window, the tulips were in full bloom.

Usually she and her father had a contest on who spotted the very first flower of the season. She hadn't even noticed the daffodils this year, much less been the first one to notice. A knock came from her door. It opened before she answered.

"Good, you're dressed. Come on. I've got something I want to show you." Mel picked up Regan's windbreaker and stood at the door as if she expected her to follow.

"I may have gotten dressed like you ordered, but I'm not going anywhere," Regan said weakly.

"Okay, if that's the way you want to play it." Mel talked like a gangster. "This is a kidnap field trip."

"Field trip?" Regan got angry. "Mel, I'm exhausted from getting dressed. What more do you want from me?"

Her parents entered the room. "There's something we think you should see," her father said.

"Are the three of you in this conspiracy together? What is this? Can't you all just leave me alone?"

"We love you too much to do that." Mr. Shaffer scooped her up in his arms like a baby.

Regan struggled. "Put me down. I have rights. You can't do this."

They carried her to the car and buckled her seat belt because she wouldn't. She crossed her arms over her chest and stared out the window. Her parents had never treated her that way.

What could be so important? Curiosity won over anger by the time they parked in front of a brown-stuccoed building fifteen minutes later. The sign read:

NEW MEXICO ARTHRITIS FOUNDATION'S HEALTH CLINIC. So that was it. More doctors.

"No—not this. I've had it with doctors. Take me home."

"It's not a doctor," Mel answered. "Just come in. I want to show you something. Mrs. Vigil told me about it. Come on."

She unbuckled her seat belt and slowly followed the others inside.

They walked down a hall past offices and meeting rooms. Regan heard squeaking, a ball bouncing, and a cheer echo from the end of the hall.

Mel opened a door into a gym and the middle of a basketball game. She led them to seats on the bottom bleacher, and they sat on the hard wooden bench.

Regan yelled over the noise, "Why didn't you say you wanted me to watch you play a basketball game?"

Mel gave her an impatient look. "I'm not playing, but Mrs. Vigil told me about this game. All of the players out there—the ones jumping, running, twisting—are JRA patients."

"They can't be," Regan said. "They're moving too fast." She studied the people on the court. They were all preteens and teens—some guys but mostly girls. They didn't all move well, but a few played as well as Mel.

"See the coach out there showing the players that jump shot? Mrs. Vigil met him at a workshop last week and found out about this. That coach had JRA as a child. Real crippled-looking, isn't he?"

Regan didn't move. She tried to make sense of what she saw. The coach wasn't crippled. The kids were active and having fun.

Mel continued, "They have swimming here—for therapy and fun—classes on how to get along with JRA; they even have their own newsletter."

Regan's mother spoke. "Maybe you could talk Mrs. Vigil into teaching a ballet class here."

"Or," Mel interrupted, "maybe *you* could teach it."

How could she teach? she thought. She could barely move. Regan watched the players on the court. Their arthritis couldn't be as bad as hers.

"Okay. I've seen it. Take me home," Regan said evenly.

It was midafternoon when they got to the house. Not saying anything to her parents or Mel, Regan made her way to her room on her own and lay on her bed.

Her door ajar, she heard her father in the hall. "Thanks for trying, Mel, but I don't think it helped. I don't know what we're going to do."

Mel replied, "She's going to pull out of this, Mr. Shaffer. I know she will. And I have one more idea."

A few minutes later, Mel shoved the door open with her foot. She balanced a stack of books and file folders long enough for her to cross the room and spill the contents of her arms onto Regan's bed.

"Are you working on your research paper here today?" Regan kicked the books away from her feet.

"The books and Internet research are for you. They're about JRA."

"Thanks anyway, but the doctor gave Mom a bunch of pamphlets already." Regan picked at the threads in the holes of her jeans.

"My guess is you haven't read a one of them, because if you had, you wouldn't be acting this way. Okay, Miss How-to-Do-It Bookworm, you're going to read this stuff." Mel piled books and files in her lap one at a time as she talked. "Get the facts. Read about just how crippling it really is, and remember you're reading about *juvenile* rheumatoid arthritis, not the kind adults get."

Mel continued, "And then if I'm wrong, and you really can't dance again, I brought another book for you. It's called *The Dance Catalog*. Read the section on alternative careers in dance. You might be surprised."

Regan looked at Mel and each book she piled on her lap.

Mel said more calmly, "You've always said that if you could find a book about how to do something, you could do it. Well, start here." She quietly left the room.

163

Regan looked at the pile of books and papers and thought about the basketball players. They didn't look that sick. None of them was like the boy with the braces at the hospital. Some of their leg muscles looked undeveloped and weak—but not all of them. The coach appeared athletic and strong. She wouldn't have guessed he'd lived through JRA.

She tilted her hips to the side and slid all the books off her lap except a newsletter titled *American Juvenile Arthritis Organization*. Regan skimmed the articles: "Searching for Clues about Juvenile Rheumatoid Arthritis: Genes May Provide Some Answers," "AJAO: Serving Parents and Children," "Treatment of JRA."

She whispered as she read, "Treatment of JRA. The disease can be controlled by the right combination of medication, rest, exercise, medical care, and a balanced diet."

Her eyes skipped to the next column. "Treatment itself may vary . . . but usually includes improving joint range of motion, suppressing joint inflammation, relieving pain, and preventing joint damage and deformity. Under an effective treatment program, children with JRA have an excellent long-term outlook. More than 75 percent will recover without major deformity or disability and will lead normal adult lives."

Regan repeated, "Will recover . . . will recover."

Taking a slow breath, she turned to the front page of the newsletter and started from the beginning. She read every article—some parts two and three times.

She read through the evening. When she refused dinner, her parents left her alone. She read late into the night. The more she read, the less scared she felt. The facts and details about JRA in print comforted her. Each book talked about recovery.

The Dance Catalog was the last book she read. Regan read about makeup, costume, and scenery designers; stage managers; dance administrators; producers; dance critics; and dance historians. Dance therapy was used to help emotionally and physically challenged children.

In the real world of dance, the one she had been working so hard to be a part of, it took more than just a dancing body and choreographer to put on a professional performance.

She read every detail of each profession. She examined the lists of related books and the colleges and courses that taught each skill.

Mel knew her so well. The books. The basketball players. More than the doctors or therapists telling her, she needed to read it and see it for herself.

When Regan had finished with all the books and articles, she picked up her dance journal. She traced her fingers over the healthy muscles of the dancer on the cover. She read through several quotes but kept coming back to one by Judith Dunn. Slowly Regan copied the quote on the page of the journal, adding in brackets a word of her own.

> **A dance disappears as you see it. A movie of a dance is [but] a dream. A description of a dance is just that. The nature of a dance includes impermanence.**

Regan closed the journal and leaned her forehead against the cover. She had wanted so badly for everything to be perfect. She had had it all planned out: All she needed to do was work hard, and she would be rewarded by getting what she wanted. Wasn't that what her parents and teachers had always taught her?

But now she knew the truth. She felt she knew something only grown-ups figured out after lots of living. She felt different inside and changed forever.

She picked up the JRA newsletter again and looked at the pictures of the kids. They knew the truth, too—and the basketball players, and anyone else whose life-plan had been hijacked by illness. She wasn't alone in her world that now included impermanence.

Maybe all along, Regan had embraced impermanence and just hadn't known it—since throughout her whole life she had embraced the nature of dance.

Regan slipped *The Dance Catalog* into the journal page with the quote, then placed both books next to her pillow. She reached for the glass of water beside her bed, picked it up with one hand, drank, and returned it. Finally, cuddled on her side, she fell asleep for a couple of hours.

But at seven in the morning, she awoke suddenly. Still in jeans and T-shirt, she cradled *The Dance Catalog* and her journal in her arms and walked toward the kitchen. Sunlight filtered into the foyer and danced around her father's ferns and travelers palms.

Regan stopped to examine the ficus tree her father had repotted. The tiniest lime green leaves sprouted all over the branches. She reached behind the other plants and carefully moved it to the front. The plant's regrowth, in such a short time after her father's seemingly devastating treatment of it, amazed her.

She grabbed a banana from the kitchen counter and headed to Le Grand Garage Théâtre. Regan opened the door to find the red, green, and blue footlights splashing their magic across the stage.

On the edge of the wooden platform sat Mel. "Your mom called early this morning and told me you'd been reading all night long."

"Funny what staying up all night will do for you." Regan slid herself onto the stage next to Mel. "It brought me a new kind of fairy. I felt her inside of me this morning when I woke up."

Mel said nothing.

"This one is peaceful and willing to accept that the only thing permanent is change, and that doesn't necessarily seem so bad anymore."

"Glad to hear it," Mel said. "I thought I was going to be a retired soccer legend before you got your tiara put on straight."

"I may not end up wearing many tiaras," Regan said. "But I'll do something. I just might have a grand career in dancing with my hands."